Sound Bites

Sound Bites

A Novel about Politics and the Media

VICTOR L. CAHN

RESOURCE *Publications* • Eugene, Oregon

SOUND BITES
A Novel about Politics and the Media

Resource Publications
An Imprint of Wipf and Stock Publishers
199 W. 8th Ave., Suite 3
Eugene, OR 97401

www.wipfandstock.com

ISBN 13: 978-1-62032-304-5

Manufactured in the U.S.A.

Contents

The Preliminaries

"Now back to Jim and more local news."

"Thanks, Sue. Well, school board meetings are rarely the stuff of drama, but tonight's was a noisy exception. Here's Cindy Howell's report."

"And dramatic it was, Jim, as parents, teachers, and administrators clashed over what might seem to be no issue at all: a reading assignment for a class of fourth-graders. But when the story is called 'A Little Bit Different,' and the main character is a boy who announces that he's gay, results can be explosive. Here's what one father said."

"Listen, I don't care if you're gay, straight, or whatever. But do we have to spill this garbage in front of nine-year-olds?"

"One mother agreed."

"They're just kids, for God's sake! Can't you let them grow up without poisoning their minds?"

"In response to such anger, teacher Nancy Nesbit defended her actions."

"All we want to do is teach our children that even though people may be different, they're still entitled to respect—"
"They're not *your* children. They're *our* children!"
"But I'm responsible for their education!"
"Then act like it!"
"That's exactly what I'm doing! By letting them know that there's more than one way to show love."

"But Ms. Nesbit couldn't soothe the irate mob. One passionate woman seemed to speak for many."

"Listen, the only teacher I care about is the Bible. And the Bible tells us that relations between two men or two women are an abomination—"

"The Bible also says 'Love thy neighbor.'"

"Does that mean you're supposed to have sex with 'em?"

"I didn't say that!"

"Hey, some people love horses!"

"Are you comparing gay people to horses?"

"Well, if the shoe fits—"

"And so it went, with no resolution in sight. Reporting from School Board Headquarters, this is Cindy Howell, *Channel 6 Action News*."

▨ ▨ ▨

"For the second evening in a row, a local School Board debated the controversial assignment given to Nancy Nesbit's fourth-grade class: a story about a gay boy who comes out. Here's Cindy Howell."

"Jim, for a while this meeting was just as raucous as last night's, and charges flew back and forth. The hubbub subsided, however, when one woman calmly walked to the microphone and addressed the overflow crowd."

"Hello. My name is Cassie McClellan. I've lived in this town for only a year, so some of you may figure I'm not entitled to my opinion—"

"That depends on what it is!"

"Shut up!"

"But I just want to say to Ms. Nesbit that as the mother of a student in another class, I respect your intentions—"

"Boooo!"

"– but you have to realize that as parents we want what's best for our children. And that's why—"

"So do I—"

"You sure got a funny way of showin' it—"

"Shut up!"

"You shut up!"

"THAT'S WHY . . . I feel that when it comes to subject matter like this, you have to be very, very careful."

"Yay!"

"I believe I have been."

"Not careful enough."

"I beg your pardon, but—"

"That's why I have a simple message for you, Ms. Nesbit. Hands off!"

"I'm only trying to—"

"Hands off, Ms. Nesbit. Hands off!"

"After that exchange, everyone seemed to be exhausted, so now the resolution of this controversy is in the hands of the Board. Cindy Howell, *Channel 6 Action News*."

※ ※ ※

"Our guest this morning is a candidate for City Council, Cassie McClellan. Ms. McClellan, thanks for joining us on *Forum*."

"My pleasure."

"Glad to have you. Now, as some of our viewers are aware, you came to public attention a few months ago when you spoke at a highly impassioned School Board meeting. Did that occasion inspire you to run for office?"

"Ben, until that night I had never even considered getting into the public sphere. But after I put in my two cents—"

"And the issue was subsequently resolved in your favor . . ."

"A couple of party leaders suggested that I become a candidate."

"Are you glad you did?"

"I just want to help our community in any way I can."

"Well, you seem to be a natural campaigner, at least according to our most recent poll, which has you leading by double digits."

"That's great news, but as we all know, it's early yet."

"Only two weeks before Election Day."

"That's true, but you know the old saying: 'In politics a week is like a year.'"

"I thought that's 'A day is like a month.'"

"You get the idea."

※ ※ ※

"Councilwoman Cassie McClellan earned a rousing ovation today as the featured speaker at the Annual Professional Women's Luncheon. Afterwards, she sat down with our Ben Hansen."

"I must say, Ms. McClellan, you really seemed to connect with your audience."

"Thanks, Ben, but I don't think such enthusiasm was for me personally. It's our 'move-on-hands-off' theme that hits home."

"You're very modest."

"Just honest."

"Fair enough. Tell me, Ms. McClellan, for those listeners just getting to know you, where would you say you belong on the political spectrum?"

"You mean am I conservative, liberal—"

"Whatever."

"I'll tell you, Ben. I don't like labels—"

"Even so, how would you define yourself—"

"I also don't think I fit any particular category—"

"I understand. Of course, quite a few observers have called you a strong conservative voice—"

"And I suppose I am. In certain ways."

"For instance?"

"I don't like wasting money."

"A lot of politicians say that."

"But most of them still throw it away on useless government projects."

"We're probably all aware—"

"And that's not how I operate, either as a member of the Council or as a mother at home. If my family and I can't afford something, we don't buy it. Even when we want a special present for one of the children, we never spend what we don't have. And I try to apply that same principle to our city budget."

"Many politicians claim to agree with you, but when they get into office, they somehow let our money fly out the window—"

"That's a trend I want to change."

"I hope you succeed."

"Thanks. By the way, if I may correct you, I don't think of myself as a politician. Something about that word bothers me—"

"I guess it does have some unpleasant implications."

"A lot of 'em."

"Of course, you have to admit that you do work in politics—"

"I prefer to call it 'public service.'"

❊ ❊ ❊

"Councilwoman Cassie McClellan has announced that she will be a candidate for State Assembly . . ."

"Welcome to the show, Ms. McClellan. Now for those listeners to whom yours is a new voice, could you tell us about your background?"

"Well, I moved here three years ago with my husband and children."

"And what does Mr. McClellan do?"

"He's a—"

"It is Mr. McClellan, isn't it?"

"It certainly is."

"Because these days you never know."

"I understand, but I guess I'm an old-fashioned girl, because I was more than happy to take my husband's name."

"Just checking. Please go on. You were explaining what he does."

"Phil is a Vice-President for Human Resources at the Crandall Corporation."

"Quite an important position."

"I'm very proud of him."

"Now, apart from your work on the Council, do you have a job?"

"You mean outside my home?"

"Exactly."

"Ben, my primary responsibility is taking care of my family, and to my mind that's a full-time career, as well as the most important one I know—"

"I'm sorry. I didn't mean to imply that women—"

"I'm sure you didn't. But remember: we homemakers work just as hard . . . maybe harder . . . than anyone else."

"Of course you do. And I certainly hope I didn't offend any of our female listeners—"

"But to answer your question, before my children came along, I did explore another field."

"Could you tell us—"

"After I earned my Master's degree in Art History, I was both a college instructor and a museum curator—"

"That must have been a fascinating—"

"It was. And I loved my work. But when my husband and I decided to have a family, we agreed that I would stay at home full-time and concentrate on raising our kids."

"Do you consider that decision a sacrifice?"

"Some people may see it that way, but for us it was simply a matter of establishing priorities. We've always believed that the first few years of a child's life are crucial. And to us nothing's more vital than the well-being of our children."

"How old are they now?"

"Emily is eleven, and Ethan is six."

"Classic American names."

"That's what we wanted."

"Both are in school, I trust."

"They are."

"And over the years you've supported them by giving time to a variety of parent-teacher initiatives."

"As a mother, I think I have that responsibility."

"In fact, it was one particular moment at a School Board meeting when you spoke urgently about a matter of . . . was it curriculum—"

"It was."

". . . which first brought you a certain measure of fame."

"I'm not sure I'd use that word—"

"That's also when the opportunity to participate more fully presented itself—"

"And that's when I realized that here was another way to serve my community."

"Commendable, indeed."

"You're very kind."

"We'll be right back."

⊠ ⊠ ⊠

"Assemblywoman Cassie McClellan appeared today at the opening of the new mini-mall on Crescent Avenue, where she spoke to a crowd of grateful residents."

"I am so happy to be with you!"

"Yay!"

"Because this wonderful place is a tribute to the power of both the individual and the community."

"Yay!"

"For a long time we've dreamed that this vision would come to life, but it wasn't until we stopped waiting for government handouts that we made progress. That's when we raised money by ourselves, found private and corporate donors *by ourselves*, and made this place happen. BY OURSELVES!!"

"Yay!"

"So I think we all deserve a big round of applause!"

"Yay!"

"C'mon, give yourselves a real hand!"

"YAY!"

"Cassie, Cassie, Cassie!"

"Run, run, run!"

"Thank you so much!"

"Run, Cassie, run!"

"Thank you! You make a girl feel really appreciated!"

"Yay!"

"And that's why I have some advice . . . or maybe it's a warning . . ."

"Hah-hah!"

". . . for our leaders in Washington and in our own state capitol. Stop throwing away our money on useless pork projects! Let us keep more of it in our own pockets! Then let us decide how to spend it!"

"Yay!"

"And I promise you that we'll do a lot better job than the fat cats!"

"Cassie, Cassie, Cassie!"

"Run, run, run!"

"Cassie, Cassie, Cassie!"

"Jim, the response from the crowd was electric. If everyone here today voted in the next election, Ms. McClellan would win in a landslide!"

※ ※ ※

"Welcome back to *Forum*, where we're speaking to Assemblywoman Cassie McClellan. Ms. McClellan, we've discussed your economic goals. But I'm sure potential voters are also interested in your views on some of the key social issues of the day."

"Whatever they want to know."

"Fine. How would you describe your political philosophy?"

"Well, I basically favor less government interference and more individual freedom."

"And what about—"

"In fact, I have a simple message for our leaders, wherever they might be."

"And that is . . . ?"

"Hands off!"

"Hah-hah! That's a phrase you've used many times before. In fact, it seems to be turning into your own personal slogan."

"If it is, I don't mind at all. It's one of my core beliefs."

"And what exactly does it mean?"

"It means that as Americans, we want to run our own lives, and set our own standards. We don't need professional politicians from Washington telling us how to behave. We also don't need media types from New York and California telling us what to think. We're perfectly capable of deciding these matters for ourselves."

"I understand. Now tell me: I've heard a lot of buzz about the possibility of your running for Congress. Is there any truth to these rumors?"

"Well, of course I'm flattered. After all, just to be considered is an honor—"

"Does that mean you'll be running?"

"On the other hand, I have plenty to do right here."

"I'm sure you do. But there's no doubt that as a member of Congress, you'd have far more opportunity to influence policy both locally and nationally—"

"I guess I would—"

"Then suppose you were asked?"

"Oh, that'd be a tough decision. After all, the position is very demanding, and there are so many qualified candidates—"

"But you must have ambitions along that line—"

"I really don't. Besides, before I take any formal steps in that direction, I'd want to discuss the matter with my family. My husband, my children, and—"

"Who would certainly play a part—"

"A big part. That's why I'll cross that bridge when I come to it."

"You wouldn't care to give us an inside scoop."

"Not right now."

"Maybe one day?"

"If my plans ever change, you'll be the first to know."

※ ※ ※

"Welcome back to this one and only debate between Congressman Dennis Buehl and his opponent, Assemblywoman Cassie McClellan. Now, candidates, I'd like to move away from fiscal matters and on to other issues. Congressman Buehl, during your ten terms as representative for the third district, you've been a staunch supporter of women's rights."

"I like to think so."

"You've been particularly outspoken on the matter of abortion. Since this subject arouses such passion, would you care to reaffirm your position?"

"I'd be happy to. From the start of my political career, I have been pro-choice, and I remain committed to that point of view. To state the matter as clearly as possible, I believe in a woman's right to make her own medical decisions. I believe that the freedom to control her own body, according to her conscience and in consultation with her doctor and her family, but especially without interference by legislators or judges, ought to remain the right of every woman in this country."

"Thank you. Ms. McClellan, would you care to respond?"

"Well, Mr. Buehl's words sound reassuring, but does he really believe that killing is a matter of individual conscience? I don't think so. In fact, I'm sure he agrees with me . . . with millions of us, both men and women . . . that we shouldn't allow anyone to kill simply because they claim that their conscience grants them that right. So let me make *my* position as clear as possible: abortion is murder. Plain and simple."

"As I said, I strongly disagree—"

"Excuse me, but I haven't finished!"

"May I just say—"

"May I finish?"

"I only want to say—"

"May I FINISH?"

"Go ahead."

"Thank you. Abortion is the taking of an innocent human life. That is my unshakeable conviction. And no liberal doubletalk about rights or freedom can disguise this fundamental truth. So let's stop trying to satisfy the selfish whims of irresponsible women, and talk instead about raising our moral standards."

❖ ❖ ❖

"As you heard, the debate just ended. Now let's go to our team of experts for analysis. Alice Lasky, what did you think?"

"Jim, for a first-timer she did a lot better than many of the so-called pros expected. Maybe they figured that because she's a woman she'd get nervous—"

"No one said that—"

"But the fact is, she stated her opinions clearly and firmly—"

"Until she became too aggressive—"

"And started whining—"

"Bruce Nolan—"

"And screaming—"

"Boy, there's a loaded word—"

"Buehl kept interrupting her."

"He was trying to make a point!"

"It was her turn!"

"And that's why many women are going to sympathize with her—"

"Ben Hansen—"

"Some women. *Maybe*. But I doubt it—"

"You have to understand."

"Alice—"

"There's nothing women hate as much as—"

"Don't you see? She's clearly wants to turn back the clock on a personal right that women have fought for decades to preserve—"

"But he's militantly pro-abortion—"

"The phrase is 'pro-choice.'

"Lisa Dubrow—"

"No one is pro-abortion—"

"It's traumatic under the best of—"

"Then why is he so enthusiastic about them?"

"Bruce, did you want to get in here—"

"He's not—"

"Her beliefs are grounded in ethical and moral principles—"

"Alice . . . er . . . Ben—"

"They're part of her religion—"

"She wants to deny women basic control over their own bodies—"

"There's nothing women hate as much—"

"She treats women as if they were children—"

"She says she wants to do away with government interference—"

"Exactly—"

"But she brings the legislature right into the doctor's office—"

"That's an exaggeration—"

"Dictating treatment—"

"Demanding that certain documents be read aloud—"

"They want to treat women like children—"

"There's nothing woman hate as much—"

"What about fiscal concerns?"

"There she sounds very convincing—"

"But without any specifics—"

"There's nothing women HATE AS MUCH—"

"On the other hand, Buehl has supported women's rights for years—"

"THERE'S NOTHING WOMEN HATE AS MUCH AS BEING INTERRUPTED BY MEN!!"

"Let's remember that."

"We'll be back to *Forum* after this message."

⌗ ⌗ ⌗

"Now to Cindy Howell at McClellan campaign headquarters."

"Thanks, Jim. I hope you can hear me over this commotion, because there's no doubt that unfettered joy is the feeling of the moment, as Cassie McClellan's supporters threaten to raise the roof. During the past week, tight polling had suggested that the outcome of this contest might not be decided until late in the evening, but from the start of the vote-counting, the numbers have been going Ms. McClellan's way.

"We now anticipate her victory speech . . . wait a minute . . . I hear something . . . and here she comes!

"Congresswoman-elect McClellan, accompanied by her husband and children, has finally arrived to address this cheering throng and relish a well-earned victory lap."

"Thank you! Thank you all very much!"

"Yay!"

"It's been quite a night, hasn't it?"

"Yay!"

"All the experts predicted that there was no way we could unseat a ten-term Congressman, but we showed 'em, didn't we?"

"Yay!"

"This is a truly victory for the people!"

"Yay!"

"'Yay' is right!"

"YAY!"

"Thank you, thank you! Now . . . I have an awful lot of folks to thank, so I hope you'll bear with me."

"Yay!"

"First I want to express my deep gratitude to a wonderful campaign team, who worked long hours every day to make this dream come true."

"Yay!"

"You were great! Every one of you!"

"Yay!"

"I also want to thank my family, my husband and children—"

"Yay!"

"Who never became discouraged and always believed in me—"

"Yay!"

"And who sacrificed their time and energy so that I might stand before you tonight."

"Yay!"

"But more than anyone else . . . more than anyone else . . . I want to thank you, my loyal supporters—"

"Yay!"

"Who rang doorbells, and made phone calls, and mailed envelopes, and gave so generously of your time and energy to carry out the countless jobs that go into a triumph like this."

"Yay!"

"And that's why I want you to remember something that's so important: this election has not been about me personally."

"Cassie, Cassie, Cassie!"

"No, it's not about me! And I mean that! This campaign has always been about US!"

"Yay!"

"Our cause!"

"Yay!"

"And the traditional values we support."

"Yay!"

"Fiscal discipline, hard work, faith in God and family, and . . . most of all . . . ?"

"Hndsof."

"I can't hear you!"

"Hands off!"

"Once more?"

"HANDS OFF!!!"

"Right!"

"Yay!"

"You and I stood together, worked together, and prayed together, and that's why we won. Together we beat the system!"

"YAY!"

"Not long ago, the political big shots figured that they owned this district. Well, not any more!"

"Yay!"

"And now we're going to take our message and our values to Washington!"

"Yay!"

"Are you with me?"

"Yes!"

"Are you with me?"

"YES!"

"Then with your help . . . and with firm faith that we are doing God's work . . ."

"Yay!"

"It's off to Congress!"

"YAAAYYY!"

　　　⊠　⊠　⊠

"Okay, panel. The elections have come and gone, and it's time for the postmortem. Ben Hansen, what's your nomination for the most intriguing result?"

"Are we talking locally?"

"We are, indeed."

"Then I don't think there's any doubt that the story of this year is the upset of a Washington institution, Congressman Dennis Buehl, by a comparative novice, Cassie McClellan."

"I think that one took us all by surprise. But, as usual, Ben, I'm sure you have an explanation."

"And, as usual, you're right."

"Never any doubt."

"Well, a few factors were clearly at work. Number one, voters were restless, and this particular outcome shows that they were prepared to expel everyone, regardless of party or experience or—"

"Maybe, but that's not all—"

"Alice Lasky—"

"I think you're underestimating her appeal—"

"What they like about her is—"

"First of all, she's a very attractive woman—"

"Stylish—"

"Bruce Nolan—"

"Young, energetic—"

"Young-*ish*—"

"Can't men talk about something beside looks?"

"Alice—"

"What they like about her—"

"And even though she was running as a conservative in a liberal district—"

"Not so much liberal as moderate—"

"Independent—"

"WHAT THEY LIKE ABOUT HER . . . what they like about her . . . is her direct approach. She doesn't speak like a politician—"

"Could I just say—"

"So voters feel that even if they don't always agree with her, at least they know where she stands—"

"Could I just say—"

"And at a time when so many candidates appear wishy-washy and afraid to offend anybody, she seems to be the genuine article—"

"Lisa Dubrow–"

"She says what she thinks."

"Didn't I just say that?"

"Could I just add—"

"But don't be fooled. This is a very smart woman—"

"Did somebody claim that she's not—"

"It's easy to jump to that conclusion—"

"You mean just because she's attractive, we should assume that—"

"Could I just say—"

"Lisa—"

"I'm only trying to point out that she's very bright and articulate, in addition to being a real charmer—"

"Are you surprised that a woman can be attractive and articulate—"

"COULD I JUST SAY . . ."

"Lisa?"

"Could I just say . . . that here is a woman to watch."

"Do you mean—?"

"I mean that she has all the credentials, plus a lot of ability, political and otherwise—"

"You think she's a comer—"

"Absolutely—"

"You think she's going places."

"If I were a betting woman—"

"And you are, or so I've heard—"

"She definitely has a future—"

"You heard it here—"

"And I fully expect her to establish herself on the national level sooner rather than later."

"On that optimistic note, we'll be right back."

"Coach, what's your prediction?"

"Biff, in big-time football games, big-time football teams with big-time football players make big-time football plays. And the Wolverines have more big-time football players. That's why they'll win this football game by at least a touchdown."

"Bammer?"

"Crossing patterns by the Vultures' backs and receivers will split the defense. There's no way the Wolverines can cover them—"

"Maybe not man-to-man—"

"A.J.?"

"Rasheed Johnson can out-jump everyone—"

"If Merrill can get him the ball—"

"That depends on the protection—"

"They'll also take away the slot—"

"That's their bread and butter—"

"Their go-to play—"

"But with a zone they can blanket the field—"

"They still can't take away the outside—"

"And Merrill can always go to the short pass—"

"But without a running game—"

"Hinson runs a four-five forty, he's stays low to the ground, and when you hit him, it's like you've hit a brick wall—"

"With his moves, there's no way anyone can tackle him one-on-one in the open field—"

"He can't get free if the blocking isn't there—"

"They've got a terrific front line—"

"But Skorianski's out at left tackle—"

"And they're not fast enough to control the linebackers—"

"Taylor's knee still isn't right—"

"Look, here's the bottom line. The game plan for this football game—"

"And Hinson doesn't have the hands to work the flat—"

"But after last week's loss, the Wolverines are a hungry football team. And hungry football teams—"

"Give me a break! Their kicking game stinks—"

"I'm telling ya'. Merrill is a big-time quarterback. And in big-time football games, big-time quarterbacks always come up big—"

"24-17. Vultures."

"He's got the arm, he's got the legs, and he's got the leadership—"

"24-17."

"The offensive line is huge, the defense is full of hard-hitters—"

"Speed beats size—"

"It's gonna be one heckuva a football game by two great football teams."

※ ※ ※

"Our guest tonight is Vance Harrington, senior Senator from our state, who's enjoying a brief respite at home while Congress is in recess. Senator, it's an honor to have you with us."

"Happy to be here, Ben. And of course it's always a pleasure to share time with family and friends."

"Thank you, sir. Well, you're in the middle of your fifth term in the United States Senate, and I'm sure many viewers are speculating about your plans."

"Ben, I wish I could give you a firm answer one way or the other, but right now that decision is a couple of years away."

"You must have thought about it."

"Of course I have, but in truth nothing's been decided yet."

"Do you expect to run for another term?"

"You say 'another term' sound as if I've been around since the Civil War."

"No offense, Senator—"

"Of course not—"

"But quite a few of us can't remember when you didn't represent our interests in Washington."

"It's been a privilege."

"And, of course, so many iconic images of you remain in our minds."

"I'm glad I'm still here to remember them—"

"Marching through the South for civil rights."

"Frightening times, Ben. We never knew if we would come back alive. But also some of the most inspiring times of my life."

"Leading protests against military intervention all over the world."

"Sadly, that's a cause that never seems to end."

"Fighting in the courts for the rights of workers."

"Another endless battle."

"Voter registration. It's been quite a career."

"Thank you."

"Plus along the way you've met some remarkable people."

"Many, many of them, Ben. I've seen this country up close, and I remain awestruck by its greatness."

"Sometimes we forget that."

"But we never should."

"Well said."

"Thank you."

"You've also seen some of the dark corners of our history."

"Let's put it this way: I've experienced my share of skirmishes."

"Recently, of course, they've been especially bitter."

"That's what some folks say, but to be perfectly honest, Ben, and speaking very frankly, passions don't run any hotter today than they did decades ago. The big difference now is the intense news cycle that runs twenty-four hours—"

"All day and night."

"Twenty-four hours."

"Nonstop, isn't it?"

"So everybody's words and emotions are a little more exposed, a little more out in the open, a little more vulnerable to public scrutiny. And one consequence is that those of us who are actually in office have to be perpetually aware—"

"Who are in the line of fire, so to speak."

"Those of us in office have to be more careful about everything we do and everything we say—"

"I guess you're on display all the time—"

"Twenty-four hours a day—"

"Seven days a week—"

"The job never really ends."

"It's a different world, isn't it, from when you started?"

"It's a different world, and it's a different job—"

"Relentless—"

"Nonstop—"

"Twenty-four-seven."

"The action never stops."

"And you're right there on the front lines."

"Well put, Ben."

"We'll be back in two minutes."

⬚ ⬚ ⬚

"The Chair recognizes Congresswoman Cassie McClellan."

"Thank you, Mr. Chairman. I have only a few questions. Good afternoon, Mr. Bogash. And thank you for appearing before us today."

"You're welcome—"

"Now, sir, you've testified that the five school districts in question are desperately short of funds."

"That's right. They—"

"But do you really expect us to believe that the money which has been apportioned to you thus far has been spent wisely?"

"I certainly do."

"Then explain something for me. Three years—"

"I'll do my best."

"Thank you. Three years ago the sum of $7 million was given to you by the federal government for the sole purpose of building a community swimming pool—"

"If I may—"

"Sir, that's an awful lot of money. In fact, it's more than would seem necessary for just about any swimming pool that I've ever heard of."

"Well, it was going to be an indoor pool—"

"Even so—"

"—with a new kind of heating system—"

"Wonderful, but that pool was supposed to open thirteen months ago."

"I'd like to explain—"

"Yet thus far not a single brick has been laid. In fact, progress has been essentially nil, has it not?"

"I wouldn't go that far—"

"Do you have an explanation for your incompetence?"

"Well, there were a few technical problems—"

"There must have been a lot of technical problems."

"—which arose because of construction codes—"

"And how about the $2 million you were given to update and improve your computer system?"

"Now wait a minute. That was completely installed—"

"But more than six months late."

"Well, in that particular case—"

"And several weeks afterwards, the entire system had to be ripped out and replaced, at double the cost, because of faulty wiring. Isn't that right?"

"Well . . ."

"Isn't that right, sir?"

"I suppose so, but there was an unfortunate incident—"

"Apparently your district is beset by unfortunate incidents."

"Well, this one occurred primarily because the company that we hired—"

"You also appear to have a great deal of trouble selecting people to complete jobs properly."

"Not at all. We make every effort to hire new firms—"

"New and unproven firms."

"Not necessarily—"

"You're generosity is admirable, but may I suggest that you're far too interested in achieving what you consider to be proper diversity through the unwise exercise of what is often called 'affirmative action' than in selecting businesses that have the know-how to spend wisely the vast sums of money that have been given to you by the federal government!"

"That is absolutely not true—"

"And now you're seeking $3 million more to start a program in international studies at several high schools, with the intention of teaching our children about exotic cultures. Isn't that right?"

"Congresswoman McClellan, in this shrinking world we have the responsibility to—"

"In this shrinking world, Mr. Bogash, throwing away tax dollars supplied by hard-working Americans so that you can achieve some pie-in-the-sky racial or ethnic balance is no solution to the daunting financial problems we face."

"If I may—"

"Thank you, Mr. Chairman. I'm finished with this witness."

※ ※ ※

"Senator Harrington, what, in your opinion, is the basic difference in philosophy between your party's view of the world and that of the opposition?"

"That's a deep question, Ben."

"I try, sir—"

"But I think I can answer it this way. When our side sees someone in trouble . . . maybe they've lost their job, or maybe they need medical care, or maybe they just lack money to put food on the dinner table, we feel obligated to help. We feel a responsibility to try to relieve the suffering of others."

"I see—"

"The other party, however, and I regret having to saying this, the other side experiences no such sentiments. Indeed, even if they see someone in profound pain, they manage all too well to ignore such pain."

"Do you mean—"

"If they see a starving child, they can look away."

"What about—"

"If they see a homeless veteran, they can walk right past him."

"I'm not sure if—"

"They figure that as long as they have theirs, then everyone else is on their own."

"But do you find—"

"Now I'm not saying that when we try to help, we're always successful. Sometimes our efforts fall short."

"For example, you voted to—"

"Sometimes we make mistakes, and sometimes the other side sabotages our programs. But at least we try. I'm very proud that we are the party of compassion, while they other side is the party of . . .well—"

"Selfishness?"

"I think that's the right word. Oh, they dress up their sentiments by speaking of 'individual rights' and 'the capitalist system' and 'free enterprise'—"

"Don't you believe—"

"—and they invoke a lot of fancy phrases to justify their attitude, but basically it comes down to this: we care about others, and they don't."

❈ ❈ ❈

"The annual meeting of the Conservative Colloquium is taking place in Washington this week, but amid closely observed appearances by several celebrated figures known to have their eye on a run for the White House, one second-term Congresswoman stole the show with a rousing speech that left this audience of fervent right-wingers standing, applauding, and cheering."

"Would you please give a warm welcome to Representative Cassie McClellan!"

"Thank you! Thank you! Thank you so much! It's wonderful to be here! Please! Thank you! And first I want to say how proud I am to share this platform with so many distinguished national leaders."

"Yay!"

"Thank you! Thank you so much! Now . . . let me start off this way. Did you happen to hear what Senator Vance Harrington said the other day?"

"Boooooooooooo!"

"He's from my state, you know, although I don't admit that fact with any pride."

"Hah-hah!"

"But, remember, he's up for re-election, so I hope you'll keep a look-out for some good candidates to run against him, so we can send him home again, this time for good!"

"Run, run!"

"No, no—"

"Cassie, Cassie!"

"Run! Run!"

"You're too kind! But first let me tell you what he said, so you know what I'm talking about! And I'm quoting now. I want to make sure that I get his words just right. He said that liberals care about people, but conservatives don't."

"Boooooooooooo!"

"I'm not kidding! That's what he said! Would I make it up?"

"No!"

"That's what *he thinks* is wrong with us. And what do *you think* of that?"

"Boooooooooooo!"

"I agree completely. Well, now it's my turn. And I'm going to tell you what *I know* is wrong with liberals like him!"

"Yay!"

"The thing is, where do I start?"

"Hah-hah!"

"Oh, they're nice enough, I guess. Some of them."

"Hah-hah!"

"And I hear they're tons of fun at parties. Give 'em a few glasses of white wine, and some slices of fancy cheese, and before long they'll be dancin' on the tables!"

"Hah-hah!"

"The problem is, they figure everybody else is nice, too."

"Right!"

"They figure that the hoodlums and thieves who cross our borders illegally to steal our jobs and flood our country with drugs are basically kind-hearted, peace-loving people!"

"Hah-hah!"

"They figure that all the bomb-makers and terrorists who want to blow us up are nice, too."

"Hah-hah!"

"They figure that all the bigots, hate-mongers, and fanatics who despise our values and our way of life are really . . . when you get right down to it . . . just misunderstood!"

"Hah-hah!"

"In fact, they figure that all we have to do is prance over and extend a friendly hand, and then. . . by golly . . . all of those criminals and terrorists will turn into good neighbors!"

"Hah-hah!"

"No, I'm serious! Liberals really believe that if we smile and tread lightly . . . "

"Hah-hah!"

". . . then give away all our resources, financial and otherwise . . . if we just welcome everyone here with open arms and an open checkbook, that the whole world will join us for one giant hug and a couple of choruses of "Kumbaya!"

"Hah-hah!"

"Am I right?"

"RIGHT!"

"Sure, I am! Well, folks, you and I know better."

"Yay!"

"You and I know that we have to remain vigilant against our enemies! We have to seal off those borders! We have to build up our defenses! We can't kneel down in front of the invaders who want to destroy our way of life!"

"Yay!"

"We have to offer the rest of the world more than a feeble handshake, a weak grip, and a limp wrist!"

"Hah-hah! Yay!"

"You know, it wasn't very long ago that the United States of America used to be respected. The United States of America used to be . . . yes, I'll say it! The United States of America used to be feared!"

"Yay!"

"But what's happened? Would you like to know?"

"Yeah!"

"Do you want to know?"

"Yeah!"

"Good, because I was going to tell you anyway!"

"Hah-hah!"

"We've surrendered so many of our core values that other countries laugh at us. They ignore us. They think we're impotent. They're convinced that we don't have the pride or will to stand up for ourselves."

"Yeah!"

"Oh, I know what the liberals say: everybody still wants to come here. Well, of course they do, but that doesn't mean *we* should *want them*."

"Yay!"

"The time has come, ladies and gentlemen . . . and I really believe this . . . the time has come to reassert American power: economically . . ."

"Yay!"

" . . . militarily. . . "

"Yay!"

" . . . morally . . ."

"Yay!"

" . . . and perhaps most important . . . (and now I'm going to use a word liberals truly cannot bear to hear) . . . *spiritually*!"

"Yay! Hah-hah! Yay!"

"Ladies and gentlemen, it's up to us! It's up to us to remind the rest of the world of a phrase that lately we haven't heard often enough: 'God has truly blessed the United States of America.'"

"Yay!"

"And you know what? It's true! God *has* blessed us! We're not just another country! We are exceptional! We are singular! We are the greatest country with the greatest system of government in the history of the world! And we know it! Now let's remind the rest of the world! And let's also make sure that we continue to deserve such blessing!"

"Yay!"

"And where do we start? I'll tell you, ladies and gentlemen: we start here right here! Right in this room! Tonight!"

"Yay!"

"Are you with me?"

"Yes!"

"I can't hear you. Are you with me?"

"YES!"

"Good! So let's get the government off our backs. Let's stop the job-killing government bills and programs that destroy our economy and our spirits."

"Yay!"

"Let's make sure the unions don't blackmail our industries into bankruptcy!"

"Yay!"

"Let's make sure we're allowed to keep the money we make!"

"Yay!"

"Let's tell all those so-called scientists what they can do with their crackpot theories about global warming and climate change!"

"Yay!"

"Because they'll do anything they can to get their hands on our money, right?"

"YAY!"

"Finally, let's keep the do-gooders and the nanny state far away from our kitchens and our bedrooms and our living rooms . . ."

"Yay!'

" . . . and our offices and our classrooms and our churches . . ."

"Yay!"

"And most of all . . . away from our wallets and pocketbooks!"

"Yay!"

"Let's work to preserve life and save marriage . . ."

"YAY!"

"To make sure our children learn what we want them to learn!"

"YAY!"

"About how great America was, how great it is, and how great it can be again!"

"YAY!"

"That's why I have just two words for those liberals who think they have a right to tell the rest of us how to live. Just two words that they should remember. And what are those two words?"

"Hdssff. . ."

"What are they?"

"Hands off!"

"That's right. Hands off!"

"Yay!"

"C'mon, say it with me! Hands off!"

"Hands off!"

"Louder!"

"HANDS OFF!"

"Once more!"

"*HANDS OFF*!!!"

"That's the spirit! That's the real American Spirit! And now it's off to victory! Thank you!"

※ ※ ※

"I was embarrassed for her."

"Those were the words of Senator Vance Harrington, when he was asked by our Cindy Howell about the much-discussed speech by Representative Cassie McClellan before the Conservative Colloquium this past week."

"I mean, this woman is bright. She's educated. But there's no doubt that she debased herself by appealing to the lowest elements of her party."

"And what might those be, Senator?"

"The purveyors of hate and fear: the twin pillars of the contemporary conservative movement."

"Do you really feel she offers nothing else?"

"That's all I heard. And that's why her performance was sad. Even sadder, though, was how enthusiastically she was embraced by a crowd that listened to her rip immigrants and workers, as well as the governmental support system we cherish, then become even more hateful and fearful than she was. Hard to imagine, but there you have it."

"The word is, sir, that she may run for your Senate seat."

"I gather as much. Well, if I ever considered retiring, the thought of Cassie McClellan sitting amid the greatest deliberative body in the world is enough to make me try for one more term. This country simply deserves better."

The Campaign

"This is a beautiful house, Congresswoman."

"Thank you. We're very happy here."

"And your children are just lovely."

"Thank you again. We're very proud of them."

"Will I have a chance to speak to them further? I'm sure our audience would enjoy getting to know them."

"I'm afraid that won't be possible."

"I understand. But what part do you expect them to play as you compete for a seat in the United States Senate?"

"At this point, I'm not sure. After all, they're entitled to lead their own lives."

"Yet you never seem embarrassed to bring them onstage with you during campaign appearances."

"As I said, I'm proud of them. They're a big part of who I am. And I want the voters to know that above all else, I consider myself a wife and a mom."

"Your family comes first."

"Absolutely."

"Although you also insist that you want to keep them out of the public eye."

"They're entitled to privacy."

"Will their status ever change?"

"I hope not."

"A few years ago, however, your daughter did achieve a measure of notoriety on her own."

"She did, indeed."

"And that episode forced her to leave her school."

"Not exactly. She decided to *change* schools. There's a big difference. And she did so strictly of her own accord."

"Now she attends a school with a church affiliation."

"Again, the choice to go to such an institution was hers, and we were very proud to support that decision."

"Could you explain the circumstances under which she left her previous school? After all, they're already public knowledge."

"Nothing complicated. She spoke out against a pervasive bias in several of her classes."

"For example?"

"She felt that her American history teacher glorified far-left positions while sneering at conservative points of view."

"Anything else?"

"She also protested when her biology teacher refused to give equal attention to creationism as an alternative to the secular theory of evolution."

"Did you support her perspective?"

"I certainly did."

"Do you believe in creationism yourself?"

"I think it should be acknowledged as a valid point of view."

"Do you believe in it?"

"I believe it ought to be acknowledged."

"But do you reject Darwin's theory of evolution and believe that creationism ought to be taught in high school and college science classes?"

"I think it must be acknowledged."

"Do you really trust the Bible on matters of scientific authority?"

"The Bible is the greatest book ever written."

"I understand—"

"It is the book on which I base the values that guide my life—"

"But do you really believe the earth is just a few thousand years old—"

"All I'm saying is—"

"Despite all the scientific evidence on the other side—"

"ALL I'M SAYING . . . is that the flaws of the so-called evolution theory, as well as the strengths of the creationist view of the world, must be acknowledged."

※ ※ ※

"Welcome back to *Capitol Currents*. Well, the mid-term elections are months away, but several heated contests are already taking shape. Brock Cassidy, what races are you following closely?"

"Roy, I'm sure we're all looking at one that's bound to monopolize a lot of attention—"

"I bet I know—"

"I think we all do—"

"That would be the long-time progressive champion Senator Vance Harrington against newcomer Cassie McClellan."

"Cassie Mac, right?"

"The amorous assassin."

"Can't men talk about anything but looks—"

"Hey, that's what her own colleagues call her—"

"Flora O'Herlihy, do you really think she has a chance?"

"Unfortunately, a very good chance—"

"Why?"

"Why does she have a chance, or why 'unfortunately'?"

"Either one."

"I think she stands a very good chance because American voters tend to buy mindless and simplistic slogans—"

"She's a very gifted woman—"

"Who talks in moronic sound bites—"

"Nicole DiBoneventura?"

"She's smart, she's charismatic—"

"Sounds like you're working for her—"

"I'm sure she will."

"The question is, does she have the political skills, the sense of the moment—"

"She has all the right instincts—"

"Could I finish—"

"Let me just say—"

"Wait a minute, wait a minute. Neil wants to get in here."

"I'd like to point out one thing. Vance Harrington has been in office for twenty-nine years—"

"Are you saying he's tired?"

"Believe me, he's not—"

"My point is that he's been around forever—"

"Only seems that way—"

"The guy's a yawn—"

"What I'm trying to say is that—"

"Of course he's tired. While she's fresh—"

"I also think the voters are ready for a new face—"

"Look, she's honest, plain-spoken—"

"I was just trying to—"

"She's also a walking cliché, right out of some nineteenth-century reader—"

"A total reactionary who hates unions, immigrants—"

"She's traditional—"

"I don't think women voters will go for her—"

"We don't vote as a block, you know—"

"Nicole—"

"Women think for themselves—"

"Not if *she* gets elected—"

"What does *that* mean?"

"She wants to think for them—"

"Brock?"

"Nonsense. She's a sharp cookie, a cool customer—"

"Sounds like Brock's in love."

"Hey, if we were both single—"

"Hah-hah!"

"Harrington is just too polished—"

"And that's just what people hate—"

"Watch. Just watch."

"And we will. So we're agreed. The key race is Harrington vs. McClellan. And the prize is nothing less than control of the Senate and the future of our country. We'll be right back."

***

"Good afternoon, America. This is Joe Lasher, bringing you a few hours of truth, justice, and the American way.

"Well, some good news on the political front. We finally have a real candidate running against that well-known liberal fraud, Vance Harrington.

"You know, Harrington, right? He's that roly-poly rich kid, whose daddy bought him everything from his first car to his Senate seat.

"He's that holier-than-thou socialist who throws away your money, that do-gooder who never met a tax hike or a government giveaway he didn't love.

"He's that fathead who coddles criminals, who always blames the cops, not the cop-killer."

"He's that atheistic hypocrite who couldn't find the inside of a church with a compass and a flashlight."

"He's that hippie-dippie, free-sex relic who probably wore sandals and love beads, frolicked in the mud, sucked his bong, passed the marijuana, and mumbled "Oh, wow" seven hundred times a day.

"Well, he may have finally met his match.

"I'm talking about Representative Cassie McClellan, known to many of us as 'Cassie Mac.' And here's a woman I really like.

"Do you want to know why? Let me give you some reasons.

"One, she shoots from the hip. Calls a spade a spade. If you know what I mean.

"Two, she's a Christian. An honest-to-goodness, God-loving Christian. And not only does she not hide her faith. She actually celebrates it! And how many people like that do you find in politics today?

"Three, she's a family woman. She has a loyal husband and two great kids, and they're with her every step of the way."

"Four, she's careful with her own money, and she'll be careful with ours.

"Five, she doesn't swallow progressive pabulum. She'll stand up to the unions and all the other left-wing factions that have poisoned the American spirit.

"Six, she puts the future of this country, our economic and military might, above all else. She's not afraid to stand up for American values, to state what you and I know in our hearts: that American is the greatest country in the world, no matter what Harrington and his socialist sidekicks would have us believe.

"Now I'll tell you one more thing, although you probably know it anyway. During the upcoming campaign, she's not going to have an easy time. There's no way she'll get a fair shake from the lamestream liberal media. They'll slam her with everything they have. So get ready for the torrent of lies, the onslaught of false stories, and the flood of vicious rumors put out by Harrington's cronies, and published in newspapers and publicized on television.

"You've seen it before. Well, you're going to see it again.

"But don't worry. We're going to fight back on her behalf. So when they declare war on Cassie Mac with fabrications and falsehoods, we'll defend her with the truth. We'll block her enemies at every turn.

"What am I saying? I'm saying that we'll do anything we can, anything we have to do, to ensure her victory.

"And why? For one reason: because America deserves Cassie Mac."

⊞ ⊞ ⊞

"This evening on *Speakout*, we'll share reflections on the state of our union from one of our most eloquent commentators, a best-selling novelist and essayist, as well as a bracing observer of the national scene, Mr. Lowry Stewart. A pleasure to see you again, sir."

"Bracing, eh? I'm not sure how to take that."

"Kindly, as always."

"Then my gratitude knows no bounds."

"Good. Well, where should we start? Anything in particular on your mind?"

"Well, I've been observing with sad amusement the Senate race in my own state."

"And your response?"

"Profound gloom, as usual."

"You've known Vance Harrington for a long time, haven't you?"

"'Nigh onto forty years,' as out sod-busting forefathers used to say."

"You're also distantly related, right?"

"Our mothers are second cousins, and he and I attended some of the same schools, albeit a couple of years apart."

"Do you consider him a friend?"

"Let's say he's more than a casual acquaintance, but less than a bosom buddy."

"And no doubt you've heard him criticized."

"I've heard him criticized, derogated, disparaged, excoriated, and otherwise pilloried by a few of the flacks who service the people that own this country."

"Now wait a minute. Does anyone really 'own' the United States?"

"The banks do."

"Well—"

"The churches do."

"Now wait—"

"Certainly the defense contractors and the weapons builders do. Manna may come from heaven, but how comforting to have a military sugar daddy."

"Be that as it may— "

"It is. "

"Fine, but how you feel otherwise about Senator Harrington?"

"I would say that Cousin Vance is an amiable hambone, bought and paid for by corporate interests. But if he wasn't, he wouldn't be a Senator."

"Still—"

"Still, he holds a few worthwhile values. And when compared to that misguided piece of stroodle who's running against him, he comes off as downright Lincolnesque."

"You don't think much of Ms. McClellan."

"Is that her name?"

"You know it is—"

"Now I remember."

"I knew you would."

"I would say that she is the embodiment of the hypocritical sophistry that passes for the conservative moral code. I might go further, but I doubt she would understand even that much."

"Could you give me an example of such hypocrisy?"

"Of course. How about the first commandment of our unspoken national Decalogue: 'Thou shalt hate sex'?"

"Now wait a minute. Do you mean that—"

"I mean that a vast portion of our populace recoils at anything sexual."

"I don't know—"

"If they imagine that someone somewhere, anywhere, might be lusting over a naked female breast, they rise up in outrage. 'Cover it! Cover it!'"

"What about—"

"If they see two bodies entangled, whether male, female, or one of each, the thought of possible copulation leaves them breathless with a 'horror, horror!' that is beyond the imagination of even Joseph Conrad, were he alive to bear witness to our collective Mr. Kurtz."

"But surely we have more than our share—"

"Of course, there's the other side of the equation: if you slice off that breast, they have no problem."

"Now wait—"

"Or if you impale those two bodies on a kitchen knife, then the forces of fundamentalism see nothing but virtue."

"Are you sure—"

"I won't even bother pointing out how we glorify violence with guns. Did you slaughter some helpless animal today? Did you dismember a duck? Massacre a moose? Then in conservative eyes, you're a real American."

"Yet we do hear outrage—"

"We never hear a peep about censoring violence. Only sex."

"Now you're exaggerating—"

"Not in the slightest. But I see surprise in your expression."

"Only because I'm—"

"Why? Such fears are our legacy. The individuals who settled this country, those refugees from religious oppression, long fabled in story and song, merely imposed their own brand of fear and loathing right here—"

"Strong words—"

"– by committing genocide against Native Americans, all the while trying to establishing a theocracy."

"You're speaking of the Puritans—"

"Among others."

"For instance—"

"I've always been amused how virtually all religions adhere to long-standing strictures about sexual and social intercourse that were dictated centuries ago by a bunch of withered, sexless males, ashamed of their own bodies and terrified of women's."

"I have a feeling you've just managed to offend a solid portion of our listeners—"

"No need for flattery."

"Were you just stating what you consider the obvious—"

"Now, however, we've sanctified these misfits and gone so far as to pretend they were ordained by some deity to set down our ethical bylaws."

"Isn't 'misfits' too harsh a word—"

"Meanwhile, these same oppressors have never had any compunction about subjecting those whom they call 'heretics' and 'infidels' to the rack, the wheel, mutilation, hanging, burning, and the countless other diversions that amused our ancestors and continue to charm millions."

"It's a world-wide phenomenon, isn't it?"

"Indeed it is. When we look at the history of the cruelty inflicted upon loyal followers of one religious doctrine by the fanatical adherents of another, only a single conclusion is possible: no animal on earth is more dangerous than the true believer."

"Would you say that Vance Harrington agrees with you?"

"I would never be so bold as to speak for Cousin Vance."

"But what do you presume he thinks?"

"I'm not sure he does think. But at least he adheres to a vaguely libertarian code that permits private citizens to seek happiness in their own way. After all, remember the celebrated, yet tarnished, emendation to the Golden Rule."

"And that is . . . ?"

"Do not do unto others as they would do unto you. Their tastes may be different."

⊠ ⊠ ⊠

"The campaign for the United States grows more intense today, as attacks by challenger Cassie McClellan grew more personal."

"Don't you just love it when Senator Harrington tells us that he understands everyone's financial problems? Don't you laugh when he says he identifies with us?"

"Hah-hah!"

"I don't see how he can. I mean, I didn't grow up with four houses, one for each season. Most of the year, when I wanted a vacation, I stepped on our front porch. And my summer home was the back porch."

"Yay!"

"I didn't go to all those fancy schools, and I didn't spend my Christmases skiing and snorkeling."

"Hah-hah!"

"When was the last time Senator Harrington actually went shopping and paid cash for a loaf of bread or a carton of milk? When was the last time he bought clothes for his kids? Why do I have the feeling he doesn't do that very often?"

"Hah-hah!"

"Somehow I doubt he's worried about paying for medical care or finding a job."

"Hah-hah!"

"Can he possibly know what it means to go hungry?"

"No!"

"Of course, he doesn't. But we do!"

"Yay!"

"We know that if you run a house, you learn the value of money. You learn to spend wisely, to get a bang for your buck, and maybe to save a little. In other words, I have a few lessons for Senator Harrington and his Washington buddies who throw out our dollars as if we have an endless supply. We don't! Right?"

"Right!"

"So what's our message to Senator Harrington and his fat cat friends?"

"Hndsoff!"

"What?"

"HANDS OFF!"

"Hands off, Senator! HANDS OFF!"

⊠ ⊠ ⊠

"In an interview today, Senator Harrington seemed to reply directly to Ms. McClellan's accusations."

"I would never denigrate Ms. McClellan's experience, but may I suggest that my years of formulating budgets for cities, states, and the federal government have provided a measure of insight that Ms. McClellan, for all her domestic skills, has not yet acquired."

"Yes, but doesn't she have a point—"

"It's easy to claim that shopping for food and clothes teaches fiscal responsibility. It's quite another thing to apportion hundreds of billions of dollars for national security when the purchases in question are, among others, sophisticated weapons systems that have to be evaluated."

"Yet she does have a point—"

"If she believes that Washington is out of touch—"

"I think she does—"

"– that sometimes we spend money on projects that may not have immediate impact—"

"And never will—"

"I agree with her! Look, I've been fighting for years against such waste—"

"And yet you yourself voted for several expenditures—"

"It happens to all of us."

"Could you give me an example—"

"Look, I admit that I've voted to fund a few small projects that I didn't necessarily support—"

"Like our state muskrat museum—"

"But you have to keep in mind that such projects were part of a massive spending bill that also brought tax relief to millions—"

"Maybe so, but then Ms. McClellan is right."

"Not at all."

"But you just said—"

"The point is, you have to understand the way Washington works."

"But should it work that way—"

"It always has—"

"And that's what she says wants to change—"

"Listen. We're a small part of a big country, and you have to get along with all sorts of people. It's fine to please your husband and children, but see how far you get when you try to satisfy 99 other Senators, 435 representatives, the President, and the American people."

�֍ �֍ ✖

"Exchanges between Senator Vance Harrington and Representative Cassie McClellan grew more pointed today."

"I'm constantly astonished by how loose Ms. McClellan is . . . with the facts."

"Hah-hah!"

"My apologies, ladies and gentlemen. No ulterior meanings there."

"Hah-hah."

"But, seriously, you've heard her talking wildly. She just throws out numbers: five billion here, seven billion there. But you'll also notice that she never quotes sources. She never offers specifics. Well, that's not how government functions.

"When she wants to criticize the unions, she might try to learn how much they're paid per hour. She might learn what the minimum wage is. She might even try to understand how many families are struggling to survive these days, how taking on two or even three jobs doesn't bring in enough.

"She'd better be glad that her husband has such a well-paying management position. She also better hope that his company doesn't downsize him right out the window."

"As if the two were engaged in a one-on-one debate, Representative McClellan struck back."

"Whenever he doesn't like the numbers, Senator Harrington accuses me of making 'em up. Well, I don't make 'em up. I go strictly by the book.

"Where did I learn the cost of those fighter planes? From the military.

"Where did I learn about the cost of the highway projects and the drug programs and all the rest? From the people and organizations that conceived the programs. They're the ones telling the truth, not Senator Harrington.

"He's entitled to his own opinions. He's not entitled to his own facts.

"And one more thing, Senator. Stay away from my family. My husband works hard for a living, a concept that's probably new to you. We didn't have everything handed to us, and that's why we don't like what's happening these days: when welfare takes the place of work, and high union wages are driving one company after another into the ground.

"In other words, mind your own business, Mr. Harrington."

❖ ❖ ❖

"Changes in campaign personnel are not uncommon, but they don't usually take place at such a crucial time, and especially in an experienced organization like that of Senator Vance Harrington. Here's Cindy Howell."

"Jim, the Harrington campaign took a shot today when Elaine Corbett, one of the Senator's key legislative assistants and campaign strategists, resigned. Here's part of her statement."

"I have enjoyed working for the Senator more than I possibly explain. He is a man I profoundly respect, and whose efforts I have proudly supported.

"But after years of nonstop work, I need a sabbatical. Thus although I shall miss contributing to a wonderful team and a great cause, I believe that this move is necessary for my own well-being.

"I know that some in the press, and especially on the other side, will look for signs of dissatisfaction on my part. But they will find nothing of the sort.

"I am leaving strictly of my own accord, and only because I need a chance to renew my own energy. I also hope one day that I shall again have the opportunity to serve my country and the Senator in some other capacity."

"Then Senator Harrington spoke."

"We are all grateful to Elaine for her extraordinary efforts on our behalf, and we all wish her the best. She has also assured us that should a crisis ever arise, she will be available to help in whatever capacity she can."

"Cindy, everyone offered smiles, and on the surface no one seemed perturbed. But did you sense any concern bubbling under that pleasant exterior?"

"It's hard to say, Jim. I'm not aware of any specific difficulties or tensions, but even so, this move is bound to arouse speculation about turmoil in the Harrington campaign."

"As well it should."

⌗ ⌗ ⌗

"We now have further word on the tragic accident in Lake Moon involving those twin girls. Here's Cindy Howell."

"Thanks, Jim. Well, the deaths of tiny Caitlin and Ronnie Turner may not have been an accident after all. Here's what Police Chief Ryan Galsworthy said an hour ago."

"It now appears that the mother, Mrs. Laura Turner, deliberately drove her car into the lake, then freed herself from the front seat and left her two little girls in the back to drown."

"Has she confessed to doing so?"

"She hasn't said a word, but all evidence points to that conclusion."

"Could you give us any details?"

"Not at this time."

"Do you have any explanation for why she would have committed such an act?"

"We've talked to many of her friends and family, and several have suggested that she felt overwhelmed by the responsibilities of caring for her children."

"Where is she now?"

"Under observation."

"Has her husband said anything?"

"Not at this point. So if there are no more questions—"

"What charges do you expect to bring?"

"That's uncertain right now. Thank you."

"Will she undergo more tests?"

"I assume so—"

"Do you think she'll plead insanity?"

"I can't say—"

"What if she does?"

"Do you intend to prosecute?"

"That's all for now. Thank you."

"Jim—"

"Cindy, it's Sue."

"Oh, sorry."

"Go ahead."

"Even after Chief Galsworthy's statement, questions persist. How could any woman, no matter how unhappy, have committed such a heartless act? Didn't anyone see any signs of how upset she was? And where was her husband all this time? So many questions, so few answers. But all we can do is wait. Cindy Howell, *Channel 6 Action News.*"

"Thank, Cindy. A sad story indeed.

"And stay tuned to Channel 6, where we'll be sure to bring you any new information as soon as it comes to our attention.

"Now over to Herbie, who has a delightful report about a pet cat who's turned into a ping-pong-playing pussy."

"I can't wait."

⌘ ⌘ ⌘

"A family tragedy has become a political issue, as two candidates for United States Senate exchanged acrimonious words over the case.

"The first to raise the issue was Representative Cassie McClellan."

"We see in the heartbreaking deaths of two children, allegedly murdered by their own mother, a sad, yet very real, example of the consequences when liberal lessons run amok. Here is a woman for whom 'doing her own thing' turned into a tragic exercise of frustration. I can only hope that this horrible occurrence will encourage us to restore traditional family values to prevent such misguided actions in the future."

"Senator Vance Harrington was quick to respond."

"What kind of woman pounces on the misfortunes of others for political gain? Not only is Ms. McClellan guilty of gross insensitivity toward a grieving family and community, but by labeling the unfortunate actions of one tortured woman as the product of more than her own private demons, Ms. McClellan reveals her own ignorance about human behavior."

"Congresswoman McClellan did not accept his criticism passively."

"I don't intend to be lectured by a pompous know-it-all whose own life is one long parade of self-indulgence masked by liberal pieties. He remains, as ever, a national disgrace."

"Senator Harrington disdained further response. Instead his press secretary released this statement: 'Senator Harrington does not believe that this occasion is a time for recrimination, but rather one for reflection and prayer.'"

"Jim, we're early in the campaign, but the bitterness quotient has been steadily rising. And it looks like we're in for a hot summer and fall. Cindy Howell, *Channel 6 Action News*."

▦ ▦ ▦

"Now to election news. And here's Bruce Nolan, who has compiled some interesting statistics for us. Bruce?"

"Thanks, Sue. Well, with the campaign in full swing, and with attacks and counterattacks flying back and forth, the results are what you might expect. Recent polls suggest that Vance Harrington is well ahead of challenger Cassie McClellan in their contest for Harrington's Senate seat. Let's take a look.

"According to the latest Channel 6 survey, roughly 57% of registered voters have a favorable impression of Senator Harrington, while only 41% approve of Representative McClellan."

"Do you think—"

"On the other hand, nearly 50% of all voters are impressed by Ms. McClellan's conservative values—"

"Interesting. Now, tell me, Bruce—"

"At the same time, and these numbers are particularly telling, according to the Wellbridge Daily Tribune poll, only 38% of voters see the state moving in the right direction. Meanwhile 42% would like to see a change in representation, but 61 % value Senator Harrington's experience and seniority."

"And therefore—"

"While, interestingly, 47% say that the state needs Ms. McClellan's enthusiasm—"

"Then what are we to assume—"

"And 49% believe that Ms. McClellan's faith guides her, while only 35% are convinced that Senator Harrington's religion plays an important role in his life."

"What about—"

"But 55% stated that they definitely do not want religion to be the most important element in the creation of new laws, while 23% said that this was not a high priority for them."

"I wonder if—"

"The breakdown is also sharp along gender lines. 48% of men approve of Senator Harrington, but 56% of women prefer him to Representative McClellan—"

"Interesting—"

"While only 38% of women prefer Ms. McClellan, but she has the support of 54% of likely male voters."

"That's quite a disparity."

"Absolutely—"

"And what conclusions do you draw from all these numbers?"

"Sue, I think it's clear that Congresswoman McClellan is significantly behind, but voters still aren't completely sold on Senator Harrington. But that's not surprising, since he's been around for a while, and people are always open to change. At the same time, the more some people see of her, the more they like her. Except for the substantial number who are offended by her no-holds-barred approach—"

"And therefore—"

"On the other hand, many voters have yet to make up their mind about her."

"They don't know her as well as they know him—"

"As we've said, he's been in office for many years, and opinions about him are unlikely to change—"

"While she's an uncertain quantity—"

"With definite appeal—"

"To a large segment of the voting population."

"Exactly."

"Then this race remains fluid."

"That's the way it appears at the moment. Furthermore, if something shakes it up, if some outside occurrence raises turmoil, those numbers could change overnight. Remember, in politics a month is like a year."

"I thought a day is like a week."

"Or a month."

"Well, if a day is a month, then what's a week?"

"A real long time."

❖ ❖ ❖

"We thank thee, O God, for thy blessings and the bountiful harvest thou hast bestowed upon our country. Amen."

"Amen."

"That's always an inspiring prayer, Anne."

"Isn't it wonderful, Reverend?"

"It surely is."

"Amen."

"First, I'd like to remind our viewers of *The Club of Faith* that this Saturday night we shall hold a special broadcast, a seminar of renewal."

"I'm really looking forward to it."

"Aren't we all? And as part of that seminar we shall include a special tribute to the new church that we plan to build when funding is complete."

"It's going to be beautiful."

"A true monument to God. And we want to encourage all our viewers to contribute as much as they can, so that the Church may be completed as soon as possible."

"Wonderful."

"Wonderful, indeed."

"And I guess, Reverend, that given our current political situation, we truly have our work cut out for us."

"Can you believe what is happening out there?"

"I cannot."

"I'm particularly interested in one Senate race."

"Which one? So many deserve our attention."

"They surely do. But I'm looking at the contest between Senator Vance Harrington, a longtime liberal secularist, and Congresswoman Cassie McClellan, one of our favorite young Christian representatives."

"We do like her."

"Very much so. You know, Anne, Senator Harrington has repeatedly voted against voluntary prayer in school."

"I've heard that."

"Not mandatory prayer. Voluntary prayer!"

"Unbelievable!"

"Even when students themselves have asked to open their classes with a moment of silent meditation, he has consistently acted to deny them that right."

"Like many so-called 'humanists,' he's desperate to keep God away from our children. I wonder why."

"I can't say for sure. But I do have a word of comfort for our listeners."

"You mean you know how they can bring God more deeply into their lives."

"And into their homes. For only pennies a day, you can keep His eternal presence on your kitchen or dining room table with this special offer of the finest silverware, which we call 'God's Cutlery.'"

"How does this work?"

"Each month you will receive a different utensil, a fork, knife, or spoon, all engraved with a message taken directly from the Bible."

"And they'll be a perfect complement to our china sets, 'Holy Flatware,' those exquisite cups and plates blessed personally by a minister of our church."

"They surely are."

"Reverend, may I offer a personal testimonial about these treasures?"

"Please do, Anne."

"I just want to say that ever since I began using 'Holy Flatware,' my meals have been more enriching than ever."

"Because now they're nutritious spiritually as well as physically."

"Isn't that wonderful?"

"Indeed. Well, we're enormously grateful to the mothers of the Church who inspired this idea, and we hope our friends at home will share in our joy."

"Amen."

"More about this offer later, Anne."

"Keep watching, and we'll provide further details."

"But first, before we pray, let us give special thanks for the latest plan to lower taxes on capital gains."

⊠ ⊠ ⊠

"Good morning. You're on WPTZ with Joe Lasher, the voice of truth, justice, and the American way. What's your comment?"

"Hello?"

"Yeah, what do you want to say?"

"Hello?"

"You wanna turn down your radio, sir?"

"Am I on?"

"YOU WANNA TURN DOWN YOUR RADIO?"

"Yeah! Hey, listen! Is this Joe Lasher?"

"This is Joe! Go ahead!"

"Is that you, Joe?"

"Yeah, it's me! Go ahead! What is it?"

"Joe!"

"Right!"

"Hey, Joe! How ya' doin', Lash Man?"

"Fine. What's on your mind?"

"How ya' doin'?"

"Just fine. Go ahead!"

"Yeah. Hey … yeah … y'know what I think is goin' on here?"

"What's that?"

"I'll tell ya' what I think. I'm talkin' about the Senate race—"

"We all are, sir—"

"Between Huntington and McMillan."

"That's Harrington and McClellan."

"Right. And this Harrison fella—"

"Harrington—"

"He's just a spoiled rich guy who thinks he's better'n everybody else just because he's got more money. Y'know what I mean?"

"I think so—"

"Spoiled rich guy—"

"You said that—"

"But that woman . . . what's her name?"

"Cassie McClellan."

"Yeah, Cassie Mac!"

"That's what they call her—"

"I really like her."

"Glad to hear it."

"I mean, she's standing up for us. She's speakin' our language."

"And who exactly is 'us'?"

"Us! White people! Christians! The ones who built this country!"

"I agree, sir!"

"I mean, all this talk enough about blacks and fags and women and Muslims. They're worried about everybody but us!"

"I know what you mean!"

"And I gotta tell you somethin' else. I've heard a lotta stuff about this guy Vince . . . what's his name?"

"Vance."

"I'll tell ya' what I've heard. I've heard that he's a drug guy, who sleeps around with anything that moves—"

"Well, sir, the rumors are certainly there—"

"And you know what else? Every time I see him, he's hangin' out with blacks. Have you noticed that?"

"I certainly have."

"What is that? What's he doin'?"

"I think he knows where his political bread is buttered—"

"Huh?"

"Well, he figures that—"

"'Cause I gotta tell ya'. I'm getting' tired of hearin' about blacks."

"I know what you mean—"

"In fact, I was tired of 'em a long time ago."

"I'm not surprised—"

"It's getting' to where . . . I mean, I turn on the television and I see a black face, I change the channel."

"I understand—"

"And I'm sicka that rap garbage—"

"I'm 100% in agreement—"

"That's not music. You can't tell me."

"I don't think so—"

"Just a lotta dirty words—"

"I've said so many times—"

"I can't even watch sports any more. I mean, all that jumpin' and dancin' and struttin'. And thumpin' their chest! Don't they know how stupid they look?"

"Not a chance!"

"And those announcers . . . they go right along with it! You now what I mean?"

"Well, you know what I say about that—"

"And just once . . . just once I'd like to see a guy playing without tattoos up and down his arms."

"Me, too."

"Looks like is a lotta blotches. That's all. You can't figure anything out. Black on black, am I right?"

"Okay, sir. Thanks a lot. I have to move on."

"Am I right?"

"I certainly see your point. But more calls are comin' in—"

"Sure, Joe, sure. Just one more thing, okay?"

"Go ahead. But make it fast."

"This guy Harrington. I'll tell ya' somethin'. This guy hates guns!"

"I know all about that—"

"Hates 'em! Blames guns for everything! Wants to take 'em away from everybody. Except criminals! Wants to take away our rights! Am I on target or what?"

"Absolutely—"

"I'm tellin' you, Joe. We gotta do somethin'!"

"We will, sir."

"We gotta bring this guy down!"

"That's the plan, sir."

"We gotta load up, put him in our sights, and bring him down!"

"I hear you, sir. But don't worry. Help is on the way."

"You think so?"

"I know so."

"Well, I'm glad. Because we Americans gotta stick together, right?"

"Right!"

"And listen, Lash Man. You keep it up, too, okay? You're the only one tellin' the truth."

"Good talking to you, sir."

"You're the only one we can count on—"

"Thanks—"

"You're the only one we can trust—"

※ ※ ※

"Jim, I've just been handed this bulletin.

"An explosion has taken place at the Women's Health Center in downtown Mattesville. Police report that the incident occurred a half hour ago."

"Thank you, Sue. Now let's turn right now to the newest member of our *Channel 6 Action News* team, Carol-Ann Tracy-Herrera, who is at the site of the explosion. Carol-Ann?"

"Jim, firefighters are just beginning to get this blaze under control, and I'm happy to report it looks like damage will be limited to one building."

"We're certainly glad to hear that. Have any injuries been reported?"

"A few individuals were trapped inside. Reports indicate that some were medical personnel, doctors and nurses, while a couple were patients."

"Any of them injured?"

"Three were brought out on stretchers, and most of the rest required treatment, but we understand that so far none of the injuries is life-threatening."

"Any word yet on the cause of the explosion?"

"Investigators aren't sure, but they are suspicious. All signs indicate that this fire was no accident."

"Why is that?"

"Apparently abortions were performed at this center, and over the past months threats have been made by radical anti-abortion forces against various individuals who worked here."

"Anything else?"

"The official word is that until more evidence has been gathered, authorities are unwilling to make specific accusations. But I don't think there's much doubt that this explosion was deliberately caused."

"Thanks, Tracy-Ann— Uhhh . . . Carol-Ann. Sorry."

"That's okay."

"Stay on the story."

"We'll have announcements throughout the night."

"And we'll be right here waiting. Quite a shock. Sue."

"Absolutely, Jim."

"That was Carol-Ann Tracy-Hernandez— I'm sorry, Tracy-Herrera. Now let's take a commercial break, then come back with sports."

⊠ ⊠ ⊠

"We start with a follow-up to the explosion last night at the Women's Health Center. Here's Carol-Ann Tracy-Herrera."

"Sue, a second patient has died as a result of injuries suffered in this roaring blaze. The latest victim was a sixteen-year-old girl, whose name is being kept confidential until the family can be notified."

"Carol-Ann, is there any doubt that the explosion was deliberate?"

"None whatsoever, Sue. In fact, police have now taken into custody a Mr. Thomas Mallard, an unemployed ex-marine who has long been associated with several anti-abortion organizations that have protested at this very site."

"Are we seeing his picture now?"

"Yes, he's the bearded man in the middle being led by officers into police headquarters."

"Am I wrong, or does he seem to be smiling?"

"We were all struck by how happy he appeared to be. At one point he even tried to wave to a crowd of supporters who actually cheered him."

"Any word on whether he's made a statement?"

"Nothing so far. But police are continuing to question him, and we expect some sort of announcement any— Wait a minute, here comes Chief Galsworthy now."

"Ladies and gentlemen, I shall not be taking any questions, but I do want to bring you up to date. The individual who was apprehended this morning has made a statement. He has admitted setting the explosive that started the fire which ultimately killed two people. On advice of counsel, he has refrained from saying anything further, but as of now he is the one and only suspect. I'll be back as soon as we have learned more. Thank you."

"Chief, any reaction from him—"

"Does he seem proud—"

"Has he confessed to any other crimes—"

"How does he intend to plead—"

"Thank you, ladies and gentlemen."

"Jim, plenty of questions remain, but all visible signs suggest the police may have their man. Back to you."

"Thanks, Carol. Uhhh . . . Tracy. Uhhh . . . Carol-Ann. Tracy."

⌗ ⌗ ⌗

"Public reaction to the recent bombing at the Women's Health Center has been swift. In fact, several pro-life groups have today put forth statements in support of the fires that were deliberately set and which took the life of two patients.

"After these statements were released to the public, Senator Vance Harrington responded angrily."

"This terrible event and the despicable words that have followed show us once more the fanaticism of the anti-choice movement. What they have reaffirmed is their utter contempt for human decency, and their willingness to kill innocent victims."

"Representative Cassie McClellan, however, had a different perspective. Here she is speaking during a campaign stop in nearby Hadley."

"While I certainly deplore the loss of life, and cannot approve of the violent tactics, I support the noble intentions of the Parents for Life movement, as well as all the other organizations working to wipe out the greatest scourge of our time. Passion in defense of freedom sometimes requires bold action, and while this particular response may seem extreme, in fact it reflects the love of every human life that characterizes the pro-life movement. We all mourn the deaths of these two women, but we ask you to remember their intention in visiting this abortion clinic in the first place: to snuff out two young and innocent lives."

▦ ▦ ▦

"Flooding throughout the towns of Brinker, Cambridge, and Glaston has reached disaster levels, as hundreds of families have been ordered to evacuate. Right now National Guard troops in motorboats are moving up the streets of this devastated community, where losses are expected to reach half a billion dollars. Even more disheartening are reports which indicate that the Clappsatony River has not yet reached its crest. With more heavy rain on the way, there's no telling when the flooding will end and what the ultimate toll will be in terms of property loss.

"President Archer spoke today from the steps of the White House."

"Our hearts go out to the victims of this terrible flood, but I want assure everyone in all three communities, as well as in surrounding areas that may be threatened by rising waters, that the federal government will do everything we can to support you in this time of need. Thus I have declared the entire state an emergency area. I'm also confident that your governor and legislature will invoke all available emergency action so that together we shall help our fellow citizens survive this challenging time. Remember, we stand with you."

"Jim, hours later the President's Federal Disaster representative, Thomas Tisdale, toured the hardest hit areas, meeting with and comforting families that at the moment have nowhere to turn, but who were obviously grateful for his support. You can see him here, examining the wreckage of one home, then floating in a police department motor boat down Main Street. One mother tried to express her desolation."

"We're just trying to save whatever . . . whatever we can. At least we're alive. But I have to tell you that . . . it's . . . heart-breaking."
"Were you glad to see the President's man here?"
"Sure. I mean, at least he's on the job. But can he build us a new house?"

"Jim, this woman and her family are comparatively lucky, because they'll be staying with her husband's parents in nearby Fort Rutledge. Still, despite all the positive sentiment, this battle will be long and hard. Cindy Howell, *Channel 6 Action News.*"

▦ ▦ ▦

"As the flood waters begin to recede, and the extent of the damage can be assessed, many people have reaffirmed their willingness to use funds from the state and federal government. One dissenting voice, however, has been that of Congresswoman Cassie McClellan, now a candidate for United States Senate. She was interviewed this morning by our Cindy Howell."

"Congresswoman, you've expressed disappointment with the President's approach to helping those victims who have been hit hardest by the hurricane and the subsequent flooding."

"That's right. I don't want to seem callous, because we all feel compassion for our friends and neighbors whose lives have been upended by a terrible natural disaster. But the President's approach nonetheless strikes me as wrong-headed."

"Don't you want the government to help these victims?"

"I want the government to do everything it can, but only within the bounds of reason and a realistic budget. Oh, it's fine for the President to offer manpower and money. But everyone has to realize that because of his misguided policies and wasteful spending, our economy is bankrupt. We simply don't have the money to throw away."

"Would you call helping desperate Americans 'throwing away money'—"

"That's not what I mean—"

"Then what would you tell those citizens who have been left homeless—"

"Petition the President. Let him know that you want him to follow through on his promises to cut those pork-barrel programs and give-aways that he loves so much. Then we can put that money to flood relief."

"But surely you understand that people need help now—"

"Of course they do—"

"Then what is your advice to them?"

"Until we see those cuts, let's ask for private donations. Let's give responsibility back to the people, who can decide just where their hard-earned tax dollars should be spent."

"Sue, we all heard those tough words from Congresswoman McClellan."

"We certainly did."

"I wonder how they'll go over in an election year."

"A very interesting question, Cindy."

* * *

"Welcome back to *Capital Currents*. And to what have been a miserable few weeks for Senate candidate Cassie McClellan. Flora O'Herlihy, how would you characterize them?"

"'Miserable' seems about right. And this *faux pas* about compensation for flood damage is just the latest in a series of blunders and misstatements—"

"She sounds absolutely heartless—"

"Sometimes there are more important things than money—"

"Or playing politics—"

"I sympathize with her point of view—"

"Brock Cassidy—"

"Because the fact is that her state, like virtually every other one, is out of money—"

"Oh, come off it—"

"Funds are available—"

"If someone wants to spend them—"

"But she has to realize that people don't want to play politics with human life—"

"Let's not forget her vicious comment about the Women's Health Center bombing—"

"It wasn't vicious—"

"It was cruel and vicious!"

"They performed abortions there. We all know that—"

"You can't just blow people up—"

"Nicole DiBoneventura?"

"They believed they were preventing murder. And if the law won't stand up to defend innocent human life, then citizens have to act on their own—"

"If we all did that—"

"Neil Gosselin?"

"We'd have anarchy!"

"Let's not get carried away—"

"But clearly her worst moment came after that deranged mother drove her children into the lake and left them to drown, after which McClellan tried to turn a profound human tragedy into a campaign sound bite—"

"Once again, may I remind you that she saw a connection between liberal policy and—"

"She didn't see any connection!"

"She manufactured something just to score points—"

"And the scheme backfired—"

"Right now she sounds like a dangerous fanatic—"

"She sounds like a loyal conservative—"

"Who had the integrity to stick to her economic guns even in a time of crisis—"

"Pure posturing—"

"That claim about money didn't fool anyone—"

"But it tells you that she is an independent candidate—"

"I prefer 'unscrupulous'—"

"That's totally unfair—"

"Would you want to depend on her for anything—"

"Brock—"

"Listen! She tells the truth. And if she offends a whole cargo of liberal sensibilities, I don't think her supporters care one bit."

"Does she care about polls? Because they show something quite different—"

"She's getting walloped in every quarter—"

"And from every segment of the voting populace—"

"Except her own conservative base—"

"Maybe, but you've got to remember that this woman speaks for an awful lot of angry people—"

"Who are fed up with unions and immigrants—"

"But if she doesn't change strategy, she'll lose even those—"

"I don't think she will—"

"I know you think they believe in her—"

"They love her!"

"Doesn't matter! That's why she'd better get organized and cut out these gaffes that make her look like a fool—"

"Or worse."

"She needs a fresh start in order to—"

"What she needs is something to shake up this race—"

"And get people talking about anything except her blunders and misstatements—"

"And what most voters now perceive as her stunning lack of compassion."

"Especially from a woman—"

"Oh, don't start—"

"Right or wrong, voters expect more from women—"

"They shouldn't—"

"But they do—"

"And that's one of her selling points—"

"Until she botches it—"

"Let's face it. She needs something new—"

"Something sensational would help even more—"

"Like what? What could save her?"

"I don't have the slightest idea—"

"Nor do I. But whatever it is, it better come fast. Or Ms. McClellan is toast!"

※ ※ ※

"And now Johnny 'Golden Boy' Tornado tosses Bruno the Butcher with a fantastic hip-lock!"

"He pulled his hair! He pulled his hair!"

"No, he didn't!"

"You're blind! It was a dirty move by a dirty wrestler!"

"But now the Butcher rakes the Tornado across the eyes!"

"No, he didn't!"

"Yes, he did!"

"Watch 'em, ref!"

"Now a kick to the solar plexus!"

"Here's the pin! One, two— and he kicks free!"

"He had him! The referee blew it!"

"And there's a chop!"

"Illegal blow!"

"And another!"

"The Butcher's down again!"

"And Tornado picks him for a backbreaker!"

"Where's the ref?"

"He's got 'em! It's over!"

"No!"

"Wait a minute! Wait a minute! Who's that?"

"Lookit that!"

"It's the Brawler. The Butcher's partner!"

"He's in the ring!"

"Get 'em outta there, ref!"

"The referee's slipped! He can't see!"

"And he clobbers Tornado with a chair. And again! And again!"

"Now he rolls the Butcher on top of him!"

"Where's the referee?"

"Great move!"

"Now the referee sees 'em!"

"He starts the count!"

"One! Two! Three! It's over!"

"The Butcher wins!"

"By cheating!"

"There's no such thing!"

"Outside interference!"

"Whataya talkin' about? The only thing matters is who's the winner! And that's Bruno the Butcher!"

"Still champ!"

⊞ ⊞ ⊞

"We start off tonight's broadcast with a shocking allegation from *The Weekly Observer*, the conservative news magazine, Amy?"

"Right, Paul. The article in question asserts that Senator Vance Harrington, currently in the midst of a close reelection campaign against his challenger, Congresswoman Cassie McClellan, had a longstanding extra-marital affair with former aide Elaine Corbett, who recently left his campaign team. Here with details is our chief political reporter, Ralph Favors."

"Thanks, Amy. Well, rumors about Senator Harrington's private life are nothing new. As many of you know, he has been married twice. In fact, he divorced his first wife after nineteen years and two children."

"Amid rumors of constant infidelity, correct?"

"Indeed. After that, he stayed single for eight years—"

"But he hardly lived as a monk."

"Not at all. To the contrary, he developed the reputation of a man who enjoys a drink or two or three in some of Washington's toniest clubs. He's also been known to maintain an eye for the ladies."

"That's why he married again."

"Right. To a woman twenty years his junior."

"And they have one daughter, now seven."

"Eight."

"Although their marriage is reputed to be a happy one."

"Absolutely. By the way, Mrs. Harrington, who goes by her child-hood nickname of 'Bunny,' is a far more formidable figure than that label would suggest. To the contrary, she's a fierce campaigner, who keeps a close eye on her husband's every move."

"She's probably conscious of all those reports."

"No doubt she is. And I must say that over the past few years we've heard very little about extracurricular activities on Senator Harrington's part."

"Although occasionally—"

"But today's issue of *The Observer,* admittedly a fiercely right-wing publication, attacks him with venom.

"Here's one line: 'Vance Harrington has long lived the sordid existence of a satyr. He is a rutting pig who wallows in the trough of sexual excess. This latest escapade with Ms. Corbett, a married woman who has been at Harrington's side for years, is just one more example of liberal hypocrisy.'"

"Rough stuff."

"Indeed. The metaphors may be mixed, but implication is unmistakable. The article goes on to condemn Mr. Harrington as morally unfit to serve in the U.S. Senate."

"Amy, this is probably the beginning of a long and ugly episode."

"I'm afraid you're right. Thanks, Ralph. We'll be waiting for more."

■ ■ ■

"Well, the conservative slime squad is at it again."

"That was just one reaction to the sensational accusations against Senator Vance Harrington. Here's Ralph Favors."

"Amy, as you might expect, reaction to this story from both sides of the aisle was swift and strong. Here's more from Harrington's longtime friend, Senator Elbert Hoffmeyer."

"Right-wingers usually scorn any attempt to protect the environment, but now they've started their own program of recycling garbage. They're replaying discredited rumors that have no basis in reality and nothing to do with the issues at hand. They've taken to slander because they lack the facts, all in an effort to save Ms. McClellan's campaign, which appears shakier every day. Members of the editorial board of *The Observer* ought to be ashamed, if they were capable of feeling that emotion."

"Some conservative voices, however, took the charges seriously. Here's Representative Martha Toney."

"If these allegations are true, and I have every reason to believe that they are, Mr. Harrington should abandon his re-election campaign immediately and surrender his seat to Ms. McClellan, a woman who embodies the traditions and family values that the vast majority of Americans support."

"Amy, we have yet to hear from either Ms. Corbett or the Senator, but they are expected to release statements very soon."

"Ralph, I know this news is just a day old, but any predictions about how it might impact the Senate race?"
"It's hard to say. Senator Harrington's long-time supporters are unlikely to be discouraged from voting for him, while Ms. McClellan's were never going to do so anyway."
"What about—"
"The big question is how the folks in the middle, the independents, will react. Until this point, they've mostly stood with the Senator, and polls show him significantly ahead. But if these rumors turn out to be true … well, this race could turn upside down in the blink of an eye. We'll just have to see."

▨ ▨ ▨

"Let me start by stating that the accusations against me and Senator Harrington are 100% totally and completely false."

"Those were the words of Elaine Corbett as she spoke this morning before a packed assemblage of press. Here's Ralph Favors."

"Amy, Elaine Corbett's tone was defiant as she denied all reports that she and Senator Harrington have indulged in an extra-marital relationship."

"Can I be any clearer? This assault against both our characters is an insult. It has also created profound unhappiness for my own husband and children, as well as the Senator's family."

"Following her statement, questions were hurled virtually nonstop."

"How long have you worked for the Senator?"

"Seven years."

"And how long have you actually known him?"

"A little longer."

"How much longer?"

"A few years."

"Do you deny that you and the Senator have worked intimately?"

"We're colleagues. That's all. Close colleagues, it's true, who have stood together for years, but just as colleagues. And to imply anything else is reprehensible."

"Do you have any idea how these rumors started?"

"We all know exactly how they started. They were spread by the opposing campaign and their cohorts in the press."

"Do you have evidence—"

"The so-called news outlet in which this vile story appeared, actually no more than a right-wing propaganda machine, has long opposed Senator Harrington and his initiatives. Now the same outlet has indirectly endorsed his opponent."

"But how can you be sure—"

"Rumors have been spread by conservative bloggers—"

"Could you be specific—"

"I'm not going to dignify them—"

"But won't you—"

"No, I won't. You all read this trash, and you know where it comes from. The problem is, *The Weekly Observer* finds these rumors and reprints them as fact."

"But if you—"

"Lies. All lies."

"Are you saying that—"

"Would any of us really be shocked to learn that the individuals in charge planted lies in order to help Ms. McClellan's cause?"

"But what about all the details in the article—"

"Coincidence. Nothing but circumstantial evidence."

"The article claims—"

"Of course we've been seen together—"

"Where—"

"And of course we've traveled together. But so have many other members of the team."

"But do you deny that—"

"What I deny is that the Senator and I have done anything wrong."

"But what about—"

"That's all I have to say."

"Amy, she could not have been firmer in her denials. The question is, will they be enough to satisfy the voters?"

"Or the press."

"Exactly."

⊞ ⊞ ⊞

"This afternoon Senator Vance Harrington mounted his own defense."

"I want to make very clear that I categorically deny all the accusations in this week's issue of *The Observer*. They are entirely without basis in fact. Of course Ms. Corbett has been a trusted colleague of mine for years. She has served the Senate and this country with distinction, and these attacks on her character are repulsive."

"Senator, do you—"

"I should also add that I feel particular pain for my family: my wife, Bunny, and my daughter, Heather. They are the real victims here. I'm accustomed to being slandered, and even such a lowdown smear is nothing new. Ms. Corbett, too, knows the score. That's part of politics. But now the right-wing gutter patrol has wounded two families, Ms. Corbett's and mine, and thereby brutalized several individuals who have done nothing to warrant such treatment. And it is they for whom I feel most sorry."

"Sir, how do you think these accusations will affect your campaign?"

"I have no idea, but I have faith in the American people, who, I am confident, will recognize these lies for what they are."

"Do you blame Cassie McClellan for these stories?"

"At this time I can't say with certainty that she herself is involved or that she has any knowledge of where they originated."

"Do you blame her?"

"I repeat: I cannot say with surety that her team, or her supporters, or both, are in some way responsible."

"Do you plan to take legal action against Ms. McClellan?"

"Anything of that sort will only give credence to these scurrilous reports. Thus I intend to continue to offer my views on the important issues of the day, and let Ms. McClellan and her cronies flounder in their own filth."

"Senator, will you and Ms. Corbett make any joint appearances to dispose of—"

"No."

"Will you wife have anything to say?"

"We have agreed that she will not dignify these lies with a response."

"Will you take any other steps—"

"Listen, I know that this is the type of story on which the press thrives. It's simple and salacious, and it's already acquired any energy of its own. And there's nothing I can do to stop that."

"Senator—"

"Therefore my only response—"

"Senator—"

"*My only response* . . . will be to do my job, conduct a dignified campaign, and rely on the judgment of the American people. They've always stood by me before, and I'm confident they will do so now."

"Senator—"

"Thank you."

❖ ❖ ❖

"Congresswoman, do you have any reaction to the allegations?"

"I've said enough these last few days, so I'll say only one more thing. Despite Senator Harrington's claims, my office and my campaign had no part whatsoever in spreading reports about his illicit behavior, or that of his associate Ms. Corbett, or about any other antics on his part."

"But you've yet to say whether you believe any of the rumors."

"Are you asking whether I believe that the Senator and Ms. Corbett actually indulged in an affair that lasted over a period of years?"

"Exactly."

"I don't know one way or the other. But I will say this: I haven't heard one drop of proof that they *haven't* had such a relationship."

"Then you believe the rumors."

"Anything's possible, and on the surface matters look bad, but I have yet to be convinced 100% that the stories are true."

"Then you're partially convinced."

"You're twisting my words."

"Not at all—"

"Maybe they did, and maybe they didn't. But I doubt that these stories were manufactured out of thin air."

"Then you believe he's guilty—"

"I didn't say that—"

"But you're implying that—"

"I'm not implying anything. Look, I'm concerned only with my own campaign, and my primary job is to do right by my constituents and the American people."

"You're avoiding the issue—"

"I'm not avoiding anything. So let me end this interview by offering one piece of advice to Senator Harrington. It's the same advice I give him whenever he tries to raise taxes or sponsor some bill that takes money away from the American people and give it to those who want to throw it away on one useless government project after another."

"And that advice is …?"

"Hands off, Senator!"

"Do you have a hidden meaning there?"

"Just 'Hands Off!'"

"Do you mean—"

"What I mean is 'Hands Off!' 'Hands off' our money, and 'hands off' anything else you feel like grabbing!"

⌗ ⌗ ⌗

"Welcome back to *Capital Currents*. Panel, what about the Harrington-McClellan race? Has the tide turned? Brock Cassidy?"

"Roy, it may have. At the moment, polls indicate that Harrington still holds a solid lead, but these rumors don't help—"

"He's down three points from last week—"

"But that still leaves him ahead by double digits—"

"Only in a few polls—"

"Most of the major ones—"

"Not the DC-AM-QT survey, which has him up by only nine—"

"But that always tilts to the right—"

"You mean it always tilts toward the truth—"

"May I just say that—"

"That depends on where you're sitting—"

"Hold on. Flora O'Herlihy, you wanted to say something—"

"The thing is—"

"Flora is speaking—"

"As long as no more shoes drop—"

"We're so accustomed to this kind of rumor—"

"We just don't know if it's true—"

"And even if it is—"

"Which it's not—"

"But it could be—"

"If it turns out it is—"

"No one's talking about it any more—"

"We're on to the next story—"

"That's your opinion—"

"You mean that's your 'delusion'—"

"But if any more reports surface—"

"I think this incident shows just how vulnerable Harrington is—"

"Nonsense! It shows just the opposite—"

"Because if he can survive this—"

"It's not clear that he can—"

"Nicole DiBoneventura?"

"Here's a man who clearly doesn't take his marriage vows seriously—"

"There's no evidence—"

"How can we believe anything he says?"

"That's preposterous—"

"His behavior over the last thirty years of his life confirms that he clearly lacks a proper moral compass."

"According to whom—"

"Neil Gosselin?"

"Those liars on the right?"

"But I'm not sure the public trusts McClellan right now—"

"Why shouldn't they?"

"Especially if it turns out that she or anyone from her team had anything to do with planting the story—"

"That's ridiculous—"

"There is no proof—"

"I've heard reports that she—"

"She knew exactly what she was saying—"

"As long as there aren't any more shoes—"

"There *are* no more shoes—"

"There better not be—"

"Maybe, but remember, folks. We're talking about Vance Harrington here. And that means that shoes can fall from anywhere."

▩ ▩ ▩

"I spent several nights with Senator Harrington."

"Those were the simple but devastating words uttered by Amber Stephens, a former member of Senator Vance Harrington's staff. She and her lawyer spoke outside the office of the Hollander Institute, a conservative think tank."

"At the time I was a secretary in his office."

"What were your responsibilities?"

"I answered the phone and did some clerical work."

"For how long?"

"Two years."

"During that time, was Senator Harrington married?"

"Yes."

"Did you ever meet his wife?"

"Yes."

"Why are you speaking out now?"

"I just want to tell the truth."

"If I may, I'm Kate Cosgrove, Ms. Stephens's lawyer, and I want to make very clear that Ms. Stephens believes that the American people have the right to know exactly what kind of man the Senator is."

"Ms. Stephens, are you saying specifically that you had an affair with the Senator?"

"Yes."

"By making this statement, do you hope to gain financially?"

"I'll answer that. Ms. Stephens is not being paid by anyone, nor does she intend to profit in any way by her honesty."

"Where did you and he meet during this period?"

"Around town."

"Were you ever seen together?"

"I guess so."

"Could you be more specific?"

"Ms. Stephens met with the Senator in many different places and under many different circumstances."

"Did any of these meeting take place in his office?"

"Sure. He has a sofa-bed there."

"Did you ever sleep in that bed?"

"Yes?"

"Was the Senator ever in that bed with you?"

"Yes."

"When was the first time?"

"Approximately two years ago."

"Did the Senator ever say he loved you?"

"Yes."

"Did he ever say he wanted to marry you?"

"I'm not sure. He may have."

"Did he make promises of any kind?"

"He told me he cared for me very deeply. I guess I thought that he loved me. I don't know!"

"But did you—"

"I'm so *confused*!"

"Did the Senator have sexual relations with other members of his staff?"

"I think so."

"Why do you think so?"

"Because I talked with them."

"Are you saying that you compared stories?"

"Yes."

"And what did they say?"

"That they … that they—"

"That's all, ladies and gentlemen! My client is clearly under a terrible strain, and she should not have to testify on behalf of other women."

⊠ ⊠ ⊠

"How much more of this nonsense must we endure?"

"Those were the words of Senator Vance Harrington this morning, as he reacted angrily to the latest accusations of infidelity that have plagued his campaign. Here with more is Cindy Howell."

"Jim, the easy assurance that we have come to expect from Senator Harrington was missing today, as he seemed barely able to control his outrage over the latest attacks on his character."

"Is the other side so desperate that they will stop at nothing? Do they intend to dredge up every woman I've ever known and accuse me of having a relationship with her? I don't know why Ms. Stephens is talking this way. Because virtually nothing she says is true."
"Are you claiming that you never had a sexual relationship with her?'
"Exactly."
"Do you deny any sort of inappropriate behavior?"
"Absolutely."
"You admit that she did work for you."
"Of course. But that's the only accurate statement she made."
"What about—"
"Yes, she answered the phone. Yes, she did some filing and other clerical work. Yes, she was occasionally in the office when I worked late."
"Senator—"
"But so were at least a dozen other interns, assistants, and staff members."
"Were you ever alone there with Ms. Stephens?"
"I suppose so."
"The she's telling the truth—"
"I'm alone on many occasions with a lot of other men and women. Some of them are young, others are older. What does that prove?"
"Do you have sofa-bed in your office?'
"Of course, but so do many other Senators. For emergencies."

"What kind of emergencies?"

"I'm not going to dignify that question—"

"Has Ms. Stephens ever been in that bed?"

"Yes."

"When?"

"One night I came back late to the office and found her there. She—"

"What happened?"

"I'll tell you! If you'll just be patient, I'll tell you!"

"Sorry."

"When I entered my private office, I found her there. She had opened the sofa-bed, taken off her clothes, and climbed into the bed."

"Was she naked?"

"I couldn't tell. I guess she wanted me to think so."

"She says you climbed in with her."

"She's wrong. All I did was sit down on the side of the bed—"

"When she was in it?"

"I sat on the *side* of the bed!"

"Then what happened?"

"I told her that I would go outside, and I asked her to dress and leave my office."

"Then are you saying she's lying when she says this turned into a sexual encounter?"

"I'm saying she's wrong."

"Are you saying she's lying—"

"I'm saying she's mistaken."

"Are you saying she's lying—"

"I'm saying she remembers incorrectly. There's a big difference."

"But how could she be wrong about something like that?"

"At the moment I have no explanation."

"Did you ever propose to her?"

"Don't be ridiculous. I'm a happily married man."

"She says you made promises."

"Again, she's wrong."

"Is it possible she misunderstood something you said?"

"Very possible."

"What did you say that she might have misunderstood?"

"I have no idea."

"Senator, do you believe Ms. Stephens is being used to discredit you?"

"That thought has certainly crossed my mind."

"Are you accusing the McClellan campaign?"

"Of what?"

"Of putting her up to make such charges."

"Not yet."

"But you might blame them."

"If the facts turn out that way, I shall have no hesitation in placing them before the American people."

"Why would they do so?"

"I think you can answer that one on your own."

"Why would she allow them to use her?"

"That's what we intend to find out. Thank you, ladies and gentlemen. That's all. I'm due at a meeting of the Judiciary Committee."

☒ ☒ ☒

"Welcome back to *Report from the Right*. Well, the news of the day is certainly the predicament in which Senator Vance Harrington suddenly finds himself. Any reaction, Nicole?"

"Just one. We've known for a long time that this man is a slimy character. And I'm not talking about his policies. Although they, too, are despicable—"

"These stories are familiar to anyone who's been around Washington—"

"I doubt that this time is the first time he's indulged his appetites—"

"I'm surprised we haven't heard more—"

"The odd thing is, he keeps talking about justice and fairness—"

"Brock Cassidy—"

"Remember, this is a man for whom the rights of the unborn mean nothing—"

"And who consistently votes to deny gun-owners their legal—"

"Everything Ms. Stephens says has the ring of truth—"

"Nicole— uhhh . . . Marie—"

"Why else would she subject herself to the calumny of the left-wing press—"

"Harrington's team says she's being paid, but there's no evidence that anyone—"

"This young woman is motivated solely by a sense of right and wrong—"

"She's been abused, plain and simple—"

"And I think she's giving a lot of liberal members of Congress reason to quake in their boots."

"Allen?"

"What's interesting is that Congresswoman Cassie McClellan has remained generally quiet about this entire episode—"

"Which is absolutely the correct move for her—"

"She doesn't have to say anything—"

"The facts speak for themselves—"

"And let's face it, she's making progress without resorting to scandal—"

"Why is that?"

"Isn't it obvious?"

"She's the one gaining in the polls—"

"Because her views clearly resonate with the vast majority of the American people—"

"She's young, she's well-spoken, and she articulates traditional values—"

"She's fiscally responsible and morally conservative—"

"Yet she also radiates optimism—"

"Her message is positive—"

"And in this political climate—"

"In any political climate—"

"Those are the qualities that the American people will always select."

"And there you have it: more analysis that's impartial and unbiased. This has been *Report from the Right*."

※ ※ ※

"Jim, legal guns were blazing today, as a representative from Vance Harrington's campaign attacked the credibility of Amber Stephens."

"Ms. Stephens's assertions are not only deceptive. They are out-right lies.

"She never mentions that she was initially given a job that demanded considerable responsibility.

"She never mentions that because of her incompetence, her duties were gradually reduced.

"She never mentions that she started in the Senator's Washington office, then after several unpleasant episodes, was given one more chance to function under less pressure in the Senator's hometown office.

"She never mentions that by the end of her tenure, she was being asked to complete only the most rudimentary tasks, but that in the process lost several vital files, and caused severe damage to the computer network that extended into both offices.

"She never mentions that when confronted with overwhelming evidence of her bungling, she refused to admit her errors.

"Thus we had no choice but to fire her, and therefore we regard these subsequent accusations against Senator Harrington as acts of revenge."

"Does the Senator—"

"What the other side has done in hauling this woman before the cameras and feeding her lines is to take advantage of an emotionally and psychologically damaged person for whom reality is only a blur."

"Thank you, ladies and gentlemen. That's all."

"And with that the press conference ended."

"Cindy, where do we go from here?"

"No one knows for sure."

"Any chance of talking one-on-one with Ms. Stephens?"

"No way. Her lawyer has her under wraps."

"So to speak."

"Exactly. But one thing is clear: this story is not going away, and we're all going to have to work overtime separating rumor from fact."

"Fair enough. Thanks, Cindy."

"You're welcome, Jim."

"And now here's Harry with the weather."

"Thanks, Jimbo. Well, the first snow of the season came a lot earlier than expected. Almost four inches in the northern portion of our viewing area. Nothing too unusual, but of course, that kind of weather always brings out the deniers of climate change."

"They don't get it, do they, Harry?"

"Nope. In fact, I have a short videotape here of what candidate Cassie McClellan had to say, as she traipsed through this freak storm."

"Where are those global warming fanatics today? Doesn't seem very warm to me. How about you?"

"Yay!"

"Naturally the crowd went crazy."

"Well, they love anything she says."

"Even when she seems to revel in her own ignorance."

"Oh, you're going to get in trouble for that one, Harry."

"That wasn't a criticism."

"It wasn't?"

"Just an observation."

"Uh-huh. Send your e-mails and letters directly to Harry, folks."

"I'll be waiting."

"In the meantime, you'd better stick to the weather."

"If you say so. The temperature right now is a relatively balmy thirty-six . . ."

❖ ❖ ❖

"Welcome back.

"An exclusive poll shows that 53% of all registered voters still support the candidacy of Senator Vance Harrington.

"41% indicated that they do not believe the allegations of sexual infidelity.

"29 % indicated that they are deeply disturbed by the rumors.

"20% have no opinion.

"23 % have not heard about those rumors.

"6 % have not heard of Senator Harrington.

"In an unrelated story, last night police broke into elegant quarters of the Berkeley Hotel on the corner of Madison Avenue and Lakewood Drive, where they discovered the office for what is said to be one of the most extensive and exclusive call girl services in the city.

"In the midst of their search, the police found appointments books and accounting ledgers that detail a network of dozens of women whose favors have been rented for fees said to range into thousands of dollars per night.

"A spokesman for the police department indicated that all these materials are being kept confidential."

⊠ ⊠ ⊠

"Welcome to *Women of the Day*. And let's get right to the big issue of the morning. Ladies, is there any doubt about our number-one subject?"

"That sleaze Vance Harrington!"

"Well, let's not convict him before the evidence is in—"

"In my court, I'm judge and jury, and I've reached my own verdict—"

"Let's face it. Here's just one more reminder that men are basically pigs—"

"That's a bit of a generalization, isn't it?"

"Does that mean it's wrong?"

"If my husband ever tried to pull anything like that—"

"You're not married—"

"I mean if I were married—"

"Has anybody asked?"

"Not recently."

"When was the last time?"

"How about during the Coolidge administration?"

"Let's stick to the issue."

"Fine. Men are pigs."

"Harrington clearly has a reputation—"

"Name me a man who doesn't—"

"Or who doesn't deserve one—"

"Men are pigs."

"And this girl Amber is clearly a pathetic figure—"

"She hardly seems to know what's going down—"

"Or coming off—"

"And now this Bordello story—"

"They're clearly trying to keep it secret—"

"Can you imagine the names in that book—"

"You want to guess who we'd find there?"

"Name a politician, and he'll be there."

"Men are pigs."

"Yet women love powerful guys."

"You mean they love rich men who take care of them."

"Not this woman."

"It's biology."

"It's destiny."

"Hogwash."

"As you may have heard, men are pigs."

"Now, who you going to vote for?"

"Harrington."

"Harrington."

"Harrington."

"Harrington."

"McClellan."

"What?"

"You're a fool!"

"That woman is out of the Middle Ages."

"She has integrity."

"She's cuckoo!"

"So you're voting for the sleaze?"

"At least he'll let me keep my freedom."

"Men are pigs."

"What does that say about women?"

"They're suckers."

"Right, but what choice do we have?"

"Well, I guess we handled that issue. We'll be right back."

❋ ❋ ❋

"We interrupt our program to bring you this breaking story. Here's Cindy Howell."

"Jim, just one hour ago, a single gunman walked into the popular family diner The Burger Joint, pulled out a rifle, and opened fire. He killed three people, two of them children, and wounded seven others. Police have arrested a suspect, one Wayne C. Aitcheson, and they are currently holding him for questioning. Back to you."

"Cindy, are any of those injuries life-threatening?"

"Several of the wounded are said to be in critical condition. We expect updates soon."

"Thanks, Cindy. To repeat: several people were shot an hour ago during a busy lunch hour at The Burger Joint. Three of them have died. We'll be back with more later."

"We now return to "Fashion Follies."

⊞ ⊞ ⊞

"How many more times must we witness such horror before we come to our senses and change our gun laws?"

"That was Senator Vance Harrington, speaking about the tragic events this afternoon at a local diner.

"Good evening. I'm Jim Smathers. The death toll is up to four now, after a man walked into the popular local restaurant The Burger Joint and shot a dozen people. Police have identified the alleged shooter as Wayne Aitcheson, of nearby Proctor. Here's what Police Chief Ryan Galsworthy said earlier."

"All indications are that this man acted alone. He has admitted doing the shooting and claimed that he was taking action because, and I'm quoting now, 'We need to wipe the vermin off the face of the earth.' Aitcheson is apparently a member of a local militia group that conducts paramilitary exercises as part of their political agenda and as preparation for an upcoming war against the United States government."

"Reaction to the shooting was immediate. Here's Senator Vance Harrington."

"We cannot continue to allow weapons to fall into the hands of every right-wing madman with enough money to buy a gun. When will we finally enforce some realistic laws and prevent this kind of senseless horror?"

"Harrington's opponent, Representative Cassie McClellan, was not impressed by the Senator's passion.

"I notice that the Senator couldn't resist slipping in the phrase 'right-wing' into his accusation. Would he have been so political if the shooter had been someone from the left? I don't think so. I am as saddened by the events today as anyone, but I also understand that there will always be those who abuse their rights as Americans. That doesn't mean, though, that we should rush to restrict the freedoms of everyone else."

"Feelings are high today, but it's worth noting, I suppose, that police have revealed that the alleged shooter had among his possessions a 'McClellan for Senate' button."

※ ※ ※

"Hostilities between the Harrington and McClellan campaigns temporarily took a more civilized turn yesterday, as the candidates shared their first televised debate. Here with a report is Ralph Favors."

"Thanks, Amy. Well, I can't say feelings were anywhere near cordial, but the more salacious innuendoes and rumors that have dominated recent headlines seemed by mutual agreement to remain off limits. Nonetheless, the chill between the two candidates turned downright frigid when the subject turned to gun control."

"Congresswoman McClellan, you've established a reputation as a staunch supporter of second amendments rights. Given the recent local shooting, as well as the spate of such tragedies that have occurred across the country, do you envision any possibility of your changing this position?"

"No, I don't. The right to bear arms is clearly articulated in our Constitution, as even Senator Harrington must admit. But every time some lunatic goes on a rampage, the Senator and others who seek to restrict gun ownership insist that the isolated actions of one person outweigh the rights of those millions who use guns only for hunting, sport, or protection. Let's also remember that Senator Harrington has admitted that he has no experience with arms. His abstinence, at least in this particular area—"

"Ooooooh."

"—should not give him the privilege of determining that others must refrain as well."

"Senator Harrington came prepared with a few zingers of his own."

"I confess I've never been a fan of guns, especially for sport. Unlike Representative McClellan, I do not find any thrill in whacking Bambi and Thumper."

"Hah-hah."

"Would our audience please remain quiet?"

"Still, I want to clarify that I do not oppose second amendment rights. What I do suggest is that we exert some governmental control on weapons used by civilians. As this latest incident shows again, do we really want unbalanced people to have access to automatic rifles? Can't we put any restrictions on anyone? I don't hear Representative McClellan object to laws that require young people to wait until a certain age before they learn to drive. She also doesn't seem to mind insisting that all drivers demonstrate a certain level of proficiency before they are given a license. Both cars and guns have potential benefits, but if used improperly by ill or otherwise untrustworthy people, both may be dangerous. I'm simply trying to minimize the danger through government regulation."

"Ms. McClellan, however, remained unimpressed."

"Whenever I hear someone invoke the phrase 'government regulation,' I know we're in trouble."

"Hah-hah."

"What we always need is less interference from the government and more responsibility for the individual. And, by the way, the big difference between cars and guns is that nothing in the Constitution guarantees any-one the right to drive."

"But the final salvo on this topic belonged to the Senator."

"Somehow I don't think Representative McClellan would be so blasé if she learned that a nine-year-old boy from down her block had stolen the keys to his family's car and run over one of her children."

"What a despicable thing to say!"

"Ralph, who would you say got the best of things?"

"That's hard to say, Amy."

"Then let me ask this: did anyone make any major gaffes?"

"I don't think so."

"And did either candidate score points?"

"I'd say they both did."

"In other words, it was a draw."

"Until the polls tell us differently, that'd be my evaluation."

※ ※ ※

"More banter about the Bordello! Let's talk politics!

"Good evening. This is Ed Crawford, and here's what's happening. The President searches for a Supreme Court Justice. Unemployment rises, housing starts lower, and the economy sputters. Finally, I'll have a personal comment about the importance of the arts in American life.

"But we begin with a story that takes us back into the gutter. Rumors about the so-called Berkeley Bordello today surfaced on several blogs. And these reports, if that's what they are, include names that are supposed to be revealed officially any day now. Here with more is Lucy Biddle."

"Ed, just how this information became public is just one of the questions raging through the city. After all, these documents were supposed to remain confidential. But a spokesman for the Police Department, Chief Ryan Galsworthy, could provide no solution."

"Those books have never left my office. Some people have suggested that copies of certain pages somehow found their way into the wrong hands, but my guess is that a few ruthless individuals are throwing names onto the internet in an attempt to bring down their enemies."

"Ed, the Chief seems right about that, because just this afternoon the Cassie McClellan campaign released this statement."

"We have it on the best of authority that among the names in this report about the so-called Berkeley Bordello is Senator Vance Harrington.

We further believe that he has been a regular client of this establishment, in addition to having numerous affairs with members of his own staff."

"Thank you, Lucy Biddle, for that report. I turn now to syndicated columnist Mark Ledbetter. Mark, you're an old pro at this stuff—"
"I don't know how to take that—"
"I mean the gossip game—"
"Oh. Thanks for clearing it up—"
"So tell me: what's goin' on here—"
"Well—"
"It's all 'we believe' or 'we've heard.' No facts at all—"
"Well—"
"Just rumors—"
"And that's the problem, Ed."
"But a lot of rumors."
"The McClellan people haven't provided details, but they figure that if they keep repeating ugly rumors, some of them will stick."
"Is it working?"
"Polls indicate that it may be effective."
"Is Harrington falling?"
"A little bit—"
"How much—"
"So far only a couple of points—"
"That's not a lot—"
"Maybe not now—"
"Is more coming?"
"I can't believe the flow will stop."
"More trouble for Harrington?"
"Let's put it this way. The steady drip-drip of innuendo is certainly not doing him any good."

⌘ ⌘ ⌘

"I find Ms. McClellan's insinuations loathsome, but all too representative of the campaign she has run."

"That was Senator Vance Harrington speaking today in response to accusations by the Cassie McClellan campaign that Harrington was a regular client at the so-called Berkeley Bordello. Here with more is Cindy Howell."

"Sue, once again Senator Vance Harrington was forced to offer denials about his sexual behavior."

"They have no facts, only gossip.
"They have no evidence, only ravings and rumors.
"They are a national disgrace."

"Sue, Senator Harrington may be right, but there's no doubt that the tactics of the McClellan campaign are having an impact. Here's what conservative strategist Nicole DiBoneventura had to say."

"Let's put it this way. Where there's smoke, there's fire, and Harrington's pants have been burning for years."

❊ ❊ ❊

"Welcome to *Sandy*. I'm Sandy Sommers, and . . . well, we've got an *amazing* story for you today! Now where do I start? Well, you all know that we women put up with an awful lot from our men. Too much if you ask me."
"Hah-hah!"
"But let me ask you this: how would you react if you husband or boy friend was supposed to be taking care of your child, but instead was sleeping with other women?"
"Ohhhhhhhhhhhhhh"
"Right in your house. With your child still there!"
"Ohhhhhhhhhhhhhh . . ."
"And doing it in your bed!"
"Ohhhhhhhhhhhhhh . . . "
"Well, that's what we're talking about today. Let me introduce Cassandra, who's . . . nineteen?"
"Uh-huh."
"And she's been married for a little less than a year to . . . Calvin?"
"Yeah."
"And how old are you, Calvin?"

"Like y'know . . . twenty."

"And . . . well, Cassandra, why don't you tell us what happened?"

"Well, y'see . . . before we got married . . . I was like . . . y'know . . . pregnant?"

"Ohhhhhhhhhhhhhh . . . "

"And he wasn't . . . like . . . earnin' no money or nothin', but I married him anyway 'cause—"

"Ohhhhhhhhhhhhhhhhhh . . . "

"Now let me get this straight. You married him even though he wasn't earning any money."

"Right. 'Cause—"

"Because he was the father of your child!"

"Well . . . "

"Wasn't he?"

"Well . . .'

"You weren't sure?"

"Like . . . he *coulda* been."

"Ohhhhhhhhhhhhhhhhhhh . . . "

"But he wasn't?"

"I didn't . . . like . . . know . . . y'know . . . f' sure—"

"Ohhhhhhhhhhhhhhhhhhhhh . . . "

"Well, let me ask you this. Did you eventually find out for sure?"

"Oh, yeah."

"And who was the real father?"

"He was . . . like . . . somebody else."

"And where was he?

"In . . . like . . . y'know . . . jail, and—"

"Jail?"

"Ohhhhhhhhhhhhhhhhhhhh . . . "

"Yeah!"

"So you couldn't marry him."

"Yeah, right."

"Let me ask this. Is the real father still in jail?"

"Oh, sure."

"And when is he getting out?"

"Like . . . y'know . . . three to five years."

"Ohhhhhhhhhhhhhhhhhhhhhh"

"Unless he makes like . . . parole."

"So that's when you married Calvin."

"What I'm sayin' is like . . . back then I thought . . . y'know . . . that my baby needed . . . like . . . a father, y'know—"

"Even one who didn't earn any money."

"Yeah. 'Cause the way I was thinkin' . . . y'know . . . I figured maybe he'd go to work or somethin'—"

"Hah-hah!"

"But he didn't!"

"Hah-hah!"

"Nah, he just like . . . y'know . . . stayed at home while I worked in the grocery store!"

"Ohhhhhhhhhhhhhhhhhhhhhhhh. . . "

"And you supported yourself and him and the baby."

"Yeah!"

"Did he at least take care of the baby?"

"He said he would."

"But did he?"

"No."

"What did he do instead?"

"He brought girls home—"

"Ohhhhhhhhhhhhhhhhhhhhhhhhh . . . "

"— and he had sex wit' them while I was at the store."

"OHHHHHHHHHHHHHHHHH!"

"Wait a minute! Wait a minute! Calvin, is that true?"

"Well . . . I mean . . . I guess . . . yeah—"

"OHHHHHHHHHHHHHHHHHHH!"

"You slept with other women in her bed?"

"Uhhh . . . yeah."

"But how could you do that while she was working in the store to bring home money for you?"

"Well, I wasn't workin' or anything, so I had to do somethin'—"

"OHHHHHHHHHHHHHHHHHHH!"

"And that's your idea of something?"

"Well, it wasn't like I promised her that I wouldn't—"

"OHHHHHHHHHHHHHHHHHHH!"

"I mean, if I was takin' care of her baby, I deserved somethin'!"

"OHHHHHHHHHHHHHHHHHHHHHHHHHH!"

"And how many women did you sleep with?"

"I don't know . . . I mean, like . . . I don't know . . . like six or—"

"OHHHHHHHHHHHHHHHHHHHHHHHHHHHH!"

"Six?"

"Or ten—"

"OHHHHHHHHHHHHHHHHHHHHHHHHHHHH!"

"And Cassandra . . . Cassandra! Now listen to me. Let me ask you . . . after all Calvin has done . . . do you still want to stay with him?"

"Yes."

"OHHHHHHHHHHHHHHHHHHHHHHHHHHHH!"

"Pardon me, but I have to ask why."

"Well, he said he won't do nothin' like that any more."

"And you believe him?"

"Yes."

"OHHHHHHHHHHHHHHHHHHHHHHHHHHHH!"

"Calvin, have you given your word?"

"Yeah. Well . . . sorta."

"OHHHHHHHHHHHHHHHHHHHHHHHHHHHH!"

"Sorta?"

"I guess."

"Cassandra, you heard what he just said. Do you still believe him?"

"I guess so."

"OHHHHHHHHHHHHHHHHHHHHHHHHHHHH!"

"Really?"

"Yeah."

"Then we'd better talk this over, young lady, because our audience has some serious questions for you! For both of you! Right?"

"RIGHT!"

"We'll be right back."

"Good evening, and welcome to the six o'clock news.

"We begin with the local economic situation, which had been showing improvement. Today, however, our area took a hit, when 1,150 employees of the Crandall Corporation received notices that they were being fired. Here with details is Cindy Howell."

"Jim, the anger was raw today when the news came down. Here's what one worker had to say."

"How can they do this to us? We've given our lives to this company, and look how they repay us!"

"How long have you worked at Crandall?"

"Twenty-seven years! Twenty-seven --- damn years! I got only a couple of years to go before I get my pension, and this is how they reward me. I hope they rot in hell!"

"That's what makes these terminations particularly painful, Jim. A lot of employees were fired before retirement, so that the company saves not only their salaries, but their pensions and health programs as well."

"Cindy, it's Sue. Any word from the union about this?"

"Not yet. And that's another reason these workers are angry. They trusted their union to negotiate for them, and they trusted the bosses to negotiate in good faith. Now they feel betrayed by both sides! At least that's what one terminated worker told us."

"They may think they're gettin' away with this, but we'll fight back."

"Any plans worked out at this point?"

"Not yet, but we'll . . . we'll . . . we'll do somethin'!"

"Cindy, any word from management?"

"Just this announcement: 'We deeply regret that this action was necessary to keep the company profitable and flourishing. We shall also make every effort to help those employees whose positions have been cut off.'"

"What kind of help do they mean?"

"No one knows, Jim. But a lot of people are waiting nervously."

⊞ ⊞ ⊞

"The echoes from yesterday's firings at the Crandall Plant are still reverberating today. Here with a report is Cindy Howell."

"Thanks, Sue. Well, the anger over 1,150 terminations of veteran employees has not subsided. In fact, it may have grown more intense."

"We trusted our union leaders! We put our faith in them, and they betrayed us! All of them kept their jobs! But we're out in the cold!"

"Sue, union leaders tried to explain their strategy, but they were shouted down."

"We knew that hard decisions had to be made—"
"Boooooooooooo—"
"The choices were tough—"
"How are we supposed to feed our families?"
"You guys aren't losing anything!"
"Management didn't give us any choice—"
"Bull ----! You had a choice!"
"We had to think of the survival of the company—"
"Boooooooooooo—"
"And we had to think of all the workers—"
"Because if we didn't—"
"Booooooooooooooooooo—"
"Everyone would have lost out!"
"Not you!"
"There wouldn't have been any company left!"

"But the workers simply didn't believe their own representatives. Here's what one man who kept his job had to say."

"All right. I'm still here. But what about tomorrow? And the next day? And the day after that? We don't have any security! But the bosses and the union guys are fine! They said they cut our salaries and benefits to save the company. But what happens when they can't pay those? Where do we go?"

"Sue, no further word was forthcoming from the company. Cindy Howell, *Channel 6 Action News.*"

■ ■ ■

"Good evening, and welcome to the news.

"The firestorm over recent layoffs at the Crandall Corporation was re-ignited today by sensational revelations on Dexter Wright's conservative blog, *Wright.Turn*. Here with details is Cindy Howell."

"Jim, ever since 1,150 employees were fired last Thursday, controversy has simmered about the negotiating role of Phil McClellan, who is not only part of management, but also the husband of Congresswoman Cassie McClellan, currently embroiled in a heated campaign against incumbent Senator Vance Harrington.

"This latest report by Wright is sure to raise the profile of both McClellans, for it suggests that Phil expressed such outrage over his own colleagues' demands for cuts in salary and pensions from the unions that management turned this struggle into a personal war against McClellan himself. At a press conference today, both husband and wife addressed the situation. Here's what Phil McClellan said."

"I want to state categorically that I worked as hard as I could for the benefit of the company. That's my number-one priority: the Crandall Corporation itself. True, when these negotiations began, I was on the side of management, because that's where my job put me. But as I listened to the debate, I could not stand by and watch the rights of workers gutted. Too many lives have been lost, and too much blood has been shed in support of those rights. I also believe that the union representatives were too quick to accept management's offer, so I understand the workers' anger with their own representatives. Thus I want to affirm my loyalty to those employees who were fired last week.

"That is why I have just resigned from Crandall. Apparently my presence has prevented the two sides from achieving a solution. In fact, my fighting for the rights of workers may have caused the Board's position to harden. If management is indeed using me as a scapegoat, my resignation might ease tensions and salvage jobs. I certainly hope so."

"Next to speak was Representative Cassie McClellan."

"My husband hardly needs my support. All I'll say now is that I know him to be a man of integrity who has given his life to the betterment of his company. I have always been proud of him, and I continue to be proud of him. And I know that I shall always be proud of him in the future. Right now he's out of work. But he'll look for a new job, and with God's help he'll find one."

"Jim, across town, the CEO of Crandall, R. Henry Carteret, had his own take on the crisis."

"Let me reaffirm that our negotiations were carried out in the best of faith."

"But not all listeners were persuaded."

"Did you carry fire these workers as a gesture of revenge?"
"Not at all. Matters of financial exigency demanded that we—"
"But was there animosity between your Board and Mr. McClellan?"
"These dealings are never pleasant—"
"Did these dealings become personal?"
"Absolutely not."
"Will Mr. McClellan's resignation have any impact on the firings?"
"I can't say for sure—"
"But it is possible—"
"As I say, I can't say—"
"But will negotiations start again?"
"As I said, it's possible."
"So some fired workers may actually regain their positions?"
"It is definitely possible."

"Jim, at this point many questions remain. The first is what part Phil McClellan played. Was he, as he claims, and as the blog *Wright.Turn* claims, devoted to the company, but someone who fought too hard for the workers? Or is he a victim of injustice?

"Second, will his personal sacrifice restart talks between the union and Crandall management? In the end, will Phil McClellan be judged as a martyr, who sacrificed his career for the benefit of others?

"Equally important, with only a few weeks left before Election Day, how will this turmoil influence the outcome of Mrs. McClellan's race for the U.S. Senate? The answers may not come until Election Day. Cindy Howell, *Channel 6 Action News*."

✖ ✖ ✖

"Senator Harrington, do you have any reaction to the recent spate of firings at the Crandall Corporation?"

"Well, of course, I'm deeply disturbed by the number of workers who have been laid off. Here's further evidence that our economy is not recovering as quickly as all of us have been hoping—"

"I'm asking specifically about the role of Phil McClellan, the husband of your opponent in the campaign—"

"I've heard that he was involved, but I'm not aware of all the details—"

"You know that he advocated on behalf of the unions—"

"Wait a minute. Let's remember that I've always supported unions. For many years now, I've spoken out—"

"But now he's resigned his position—"

"So I understand. Apparently he was in the way—"

"He negotiated too strongly—"

"I heard that he was out of control—"

"But now he says he wants to help recover jobs that have been lost—"

"That's certainly noble of him."

"Are you mocking him, Senator?"

"Certainly not—"

"Are you laughing about the lost jobs?"

"Of course not—"

"Do you think his resignation will make a difference?"

"I can't say with certainty. I myself have been making inquiries to see if I can personally offer advice or assistance—"

"Isn't this a little late to become involved—"

"I wouldn't say so, no. There's still time—"

"Not a lot, sir."

"Even so, I wish Mr. McClellan luck. May I also suggest that perhaps Mrs. McClellan should finally—"

"The Congresswoman."

"Indeed. The Congresswoman."

"We've heard reports that she's been offering all the assistance she can."

"I haven't heard anything to that effect."

"She's supposedly working behind the scenes."

"That's fine, but maybe the time has come for her to put forward a jobs plan of her own to help workers all over the state, rather than just criticize those of us who have been working for years to get this economy rolling again."

"She's definitely involved at Crandall—"

"She may be—"

"At least that's what we're told—"

"In the meantime I've put out a five-point plan for growth—"

"Sorry, Senator. We're out of time."

⌘ ⌘ ⌘

"Congresswoman, what's your reaction to Senator Harrington's comments?"

"They're what I would expect."

"What do you mean?"

"Has this state ever been burdened with a more ineffectual public servant?"

"I don't know if I'd call him ineffec—"

"Here's a man who's never done a lick of real work in his life, never held a real job, just run for office—"

"That's quite a claim—"

"And now, when millions of hard-working Americans are fighting for their livelihood, fighting to feed their families, he sits on the sidelines and takes potshots."

"He insists he's tried to support negotiations."

"Have you seen any evidence of help from him?"

"Not yet."

"Neither has anybody else."

"Of course—"

"Meanwhile, my husband has spent months battling corporate forces, and now he's sacrificed his own job so that others can retain theirs."

"Senator Harrington accuses you of being a puppet of corporate interests."

"Does he have any idea what's going on?"

"He blames you for trying to protect their tax loopholes—"

"These are the people who create jobs. I want to help them."

"But are you willing to increase any taxes at all—"

"Let me repeat the truth. My husband lost his job fighting for working men and women. I don't know what planet Senator Harrington is coming from, but for a guy who's profited his whole life from all those supposed tax loopholes, he's suddenly singing an entirely new tune."

"But would you ever raise taxes—"

"So let's not hear any more from Mr. Harrington about his deep sympathy for those of us who work for a living."

"You must be proud of your husband."

"I certainly am. Very proud."

"And what about Senator Harrington?"

"I don't know what to say about him. Wait a minute. Yes, I do know what to say. I'm embarrassed for him. I'm embarrassed, and I'm ashamed."

▦ ▦ ▦

"Welcome back to *Capital Currents*.

"Issue two: Firing Fiasco!

"Massive layoffs at the Crandall Corporation became the subject of greater controversy, when allegations arose that Phil McClellan, wife of Senatorial candidate Cassie McClellan, was forced by management to resign his own executive position as part of a settlement by which workers could regain jobs. Brock Cassidy, your reaction?"

"Roy, this can only be good news for the McClellan campaign. She's never been a favorite of the union guys—"

"You mean she's made it very clear that she hates them—"

"Which is why they hate her—"

"She's spits on the unions—"

"But in a time of economic downtown, even the possibility that her husband sacrificed his job so that others could have theirs—"

"But we have to consider the source of the story—"

"Just because it's a conservative blog doesn't mean that the report isn't true—"

"Neil Gosselin—"

"Dexter Wright is a kook of the first order—"

"He is a respected journalist—"

"He has ties with a number of fanatical groups that have been on the government's list of dangerous organizations—"

"That doesn't prove a thing—"

"Just last year he was accused of bugging the homes of several reporters—"

"He was accused! Not convicted!"

"As well as hacking their phones—"

"Stop making up stories!"

"He admitted he did it!"

"Let's face it. Mr. Wright has been known to tell a good many whoppers—"

"As well as a lot of scoops—"

"This one doesn't pass the smell test—"

"Has anyone denied anything? Has management denied the report—"

"Not yet. But that doesn't mean I believe them—"

"Then you're one of the very few—"

"That may be the case among the lefties—"

"There are suspicions all over—"

"Let's stick to the issue. The downside may be the loss of 1,150 jobs, but the upside for the McClellan campaign is that since she has long claimed that she fights for the average citizen—"

"Another fair tale—"

"Be that as it may—"

"Nicole DiBoneventura?"

"The crux of the matter is that his quitting comes off as downright courageous."

"If you believe his tale."

"As a lot of people clearly do."

"A lot don't!"

"Sounds like another Reagan to me."

"What's that supposed to mean?"

"Neil Gosselin?"

"You know exactly what it means. When he was Head of the Actors Union, Reagan betrayed his fellow members and made a deal with the studios—"

"That is an absolute lie—"

"Complete falsehood—"

"An arrangement that marked the beginning of his career in politics."

"Thanks to a lot of sordid characters—"

"Do you just make up these things?"

"Look, I know that in your mind he's still St. Ronald of Reagan—"

"It's a lie!"

"Just read the history, all right?"

"May I remind you that the issue remains: how much does the McClellan campaign benefit from—"

"And the answer is plenty—"

"She's been steadily making up ground—"

"She's still behind—"

"Not for long—"

"The thing is, Harrington has been fighting for workers for decades—"

"He's always been on the side of the unions—"

"You mean he's in their back pocket."

"As opposed to corporate interests—"

"But right now he sounds like a bitter old man whose ravings don't amount to—"

"All he can do is sit there and mock both McClellans. And everyone knows it."

"That's not helping—"

"What about her? All this phony compassion—"

"She just got into the act—"

"She needs something else. This report alone won't do it."

"But it'll help."

"Maybe."

"Unless we learn that it's a total fabrication."

"Which it isn't."

"Does anyone want to take bets about that?"

"Just wait until election day."

"Do we have a choice?"

"That's the only contest that matters."

▨ ▨ ▨

"We start off tonight's news with politics.

"It's been a couple of weeks since we heard the name 'Amber Stephens,' but last night the internet overflowed with messages sent to this one-time campaign worker by her former boss, Senator Vance Harrington. Here's Cindy Howell."

"Jim, I don't know if I'd use the word 'sensational,' but that's the way a couple of spokespersons for the McClellan campaign have described this collection of twitter and e-mail records released yesterday evening by Ms. Stephens.

"One of them reads as follows: 'I shall never forget last night. You were absolutely wonderful.'

"Today the doe-eyed Ms. Stephens faced the press to explain her decision to violate the confidential nature of her relationship with the Senator."

"The world should know the kind of man Senator Vance Harrington is. For the last few weeks, he has made accusations against me. Well, my self-respect demands that I answer his wild remarks."

"Are you trying to take revenge against him?"

"I'm telling the truth."

"Does this message refer to a romantic episode with the Senator?"

"It refers to a night we spent in his office."

"How long ago did this night take place?"

"A year and a half ago."

"Why have you waited so long to release the information?"

"I didn't want to bring any more scandal to either one of us."

"Would you like to see Senator Harrington lose this election?"

"I'd be very happy."

"Do you have any more letters or e-mails?"

"I have lots of stuff."

"Do you have pictures?"

"I have lots of everything."

"Will you release more of it?"

"If I think it's necessary."

"Then Kate Cosgrove, Ms. Stephens's lawyer, spoke."

"Ladies and gentlemen, as Ms. Stephens indicated, she feels obliged to defend herself against defamatory statements from the Harrington campaign. She takes no pleasure in creating this spectacle, for the material she has released debases not only the man, but the office he holds and the country he supposedly serves. However, Ms. Stephens believes that for many reasons she has no choice. Thank you."

"Will she tell more—"?
"What does she want—"
"When will she—"
"That's all."
"But when—"
"That's all."

"And then Ms. Stephens was gone. Jim, her game plan is clear. She tantalizes us with a few tidbits, then leaves the press to scrounge for more."

"And the strategy seems to be working."

"It just may be. Either way, the ball is now in Senator Harrington's court, and he'll have to respond to what are clearly powerful allegations. Cindy Howell, *Channel 6 Action News*."

"Thank you, Cindy. Wow. Quite a story."
"Could this news tilt an election?"
"It might."
"And with it the balance of power in the Senate."

✖ ✖ ✖

"Once again, in a desperate attempt to smear me personally and to undermine our campaign, the McClellan organization has thrown in front of us a compendium of lies and distortions."

"That was Senator Vance Harrington speaking today at a hastily called news conference, canceling other obligations to confront further allegations of infidelity and other inappropriate behavior.

"Good evening, and welcome to the six o'clock news. I'm Jim Smathers."

"And I'm Sue Konstacky. Here with details of that extraordinary event today is Cindy Howell."

"Thanks, Sue. Well, the knives were out again this afternoon, as Senator Vance Harrington was once more forced to defend himself against accusations by his opponent, Cassie McClellan."

"Congresswoman McClellan has once again lowered this campaign into the gutter. She has gotten her hands on private communications, then purposefully distorted them, all in an attempt to smear me and my colleagues."

"Did you send that e-mail?"

"Yes, I did—"

"Ohhhhh . . ."

"But I sent the same one to a dozen other staff members who worked late that same evening."

"What kind of work—"

"We were turning out correspondence, as well as position papers and other policy documents. The entire team made an extra effort. That e-mail was simply my expression of gratitude."

"Sir, did you—"

"If you read carefully, you will notice that all these memos are simply statements of thanks. Thus despite the efforts of the McClellan organization to bring out the worst possible interpretation, these documents contain nothing salacious, nothing smutty, nothing even remotely illegal. The immorality the McClellan team pretends to find is simply the product of their own fevered imaginations."

"A spokesman for the McClellan campaign offered this brief response."

"The Senator speaks of "position papers." I can only begin to guess at what 'positions' he's talking about.

"We believe Ms. Stephens when she says that she and the Senator were romantically involved. In light of this newly released correspondence, his contorted denials ring hollow indeed."

"Sue, it's charge and countercharge. Back to you."

⊞ ⊞ ⊞

"Hey, welcome back to the big show, kids. In a little while, we'll meet the always lovely, always dazzling, always amusing . . . Jennifer . . . Jessica . . . "

"Jennifer."

"That's right. Jennifer! I knew it all the time. Hah-hah!"

"Hah-hah!"

"Anyway, some actress will walk out here. And she'll be beautiful and charming! But before she does, I now hold in my hands tonight's Top Ten List."

"Yay!"

"Listen, I'm sure everybody knows that President Archer is having a tough time filling his latest Supreme Court vacancy. Have you heard that, Hank?"

"I definitely have."

"We'll it's been in all the papers."

"That's probably where I read it."

"Do you read the papers?"

"Every day."

"Then that's probably where you read it."

"That's what I said."

"Oh! I guess I wasn't listening. Hah-hah!"

"Hah-hah!"

"Anyway, try to follow me on this. We've got eight judges. But we need nine. We've got eight. But we need nine. They're got their robes, they're seated at that thing . . . what do they call that thing where they sit?"

"The platform?"

"No!'

"The dais?"

"The *dais*? What's that?"

"I don't know. You asked me!"

"And you don't know."

"Right!"

"I don't, either! Hah-hah!"

"Hah-hah!"

"Anyway, these eight judges, they're ready to go. They're ready for action. But for the Court to work, we need nine. Otherwise, the Court can't function. Can you follow me?"

"Every step of the way."

"We've got eight. But we need nine. You know what that means, Hank?"

"What?"

"We're one Supreme short! Hah-hah!"

"Ah, hah-hah! Is that like one Pip?"

"I don't know! Hah-hah!"

"Hah-hah!"

"Anyway, here's tonight's Top Ten List: 'Ten Reasons Why the President's Latest Nominee Didn't Make It.

"Number 10: He ran into his confirmation hearing and shouted 'Here Come Da' Judge.

"Number 9: Every time someone yells 'Order in the Court,' he shouts 'More Fries!'

"Number 8: Whenever someone asks to see his briefs, he opens his robes.

"Number 7: They won't let him borrow the evidence at pornography trials.

"Number 6: He keeps calling the First Lady 'The Un-indicted Co-Conspirator.'

"Number 5: He offered to show the Committee new examples of judicial restraint. HEY, WHAT DOES THAT MEAN!?

"Number 4: He revealed that the President's Secret Service Code name is Bozo.

"Number 3: He told the Attorney General to moon the Court.

"Number 2: He refuses to okay Congressional Strip Searches.

"Number 1: And the Number 1 reason why President Archer's latest Supreme Court nominee is in trouble . . . He keeps asking to play with everyone's gavel!

⊞ ⊞ ⊞

"Now to political news, and the latest polling in the tightly contested Senate race.

"Senator Vance Harrington remains slightly ahead of challenger Cassie McClellan by 49% to 44%, with a margin of error of 4%.

"In other words, the race continues to tighten."

"Right, Jim. Apparently the allegations of infidelity have hurt the Senator, while Congresswoman McClellan's numbers have been helped by her husband's role in the employment wars at the Crandall Corporation."

"Two weeks to go, and it's anybody's ballgame."

"Apparently so."

"We'll be watching."

"Meanwhile, Jim, police are looking for evidence in a break-in that occurred last night at the downtown medical office of Dr. Simon Lannahan, a prominent psychiatrist. A whole batch of records were stolen, and no one is quite sure why. Here's Chief Ryan Galsworthy responding to questions."

"The doctor had a good many celebrity clients, right?"
"He certainly did."
"Are you considering the possibility of blackmail?"
"Definitely."
"Any clues as to when the break-in took place?"
"All the evidence suggests that it occurred sometime late last night or very early this morning."
"Any idea as to the number of files stolen?"
"Not at this time. The doctor is currently trying to provide us with that information."
"Were any medicines, drugs, or other such materials missing?"
"Apparently not."
"Just records."
"So it seems."
"Any speculation as to why these records in particular were taken?"
"Not at this point."
"Do you see any pattern whatsoever?"
"Not at this point."

"Welcome back to *Inside Entertainment*.

"Well, just three days ago, a judge granted Veronica Nostrand freedom to serve out her days of community service from home, but last night the irrepressible twenty-three-year-old superstar was hitting the bar scene in downtown LA at the newest nighttime hot spot, 'Middle Earth.'

"Here's our Lloyd La Chasse."

"Christie, in her own words, 'Ver-no never says no,' as she danced and drank the night away.

"Here you see her entering the bar, waving kisses to fans, as the paparazzi flashed the cameras, and the wild child flashed them right back.

If she was wearing underwear beneath that micro-mini with the see-through top, no one saw it."

"Lloyd, did you have a chance to talk to her?"

"I did ask one question about rumors that she had just been fired from her latest movie, which is scheduled to begin shooting next month, but she just laughed. Maybe she didn't hear me. Either way, if she's worried about the judge's warning that she might go to prison for her latest drunk-driving escapade, she didn't show it last night."

"Can you tell us what time she left?"

"Here she is leaving the club at about 2 a.m. Someone shouted she had drunk too much to drive, but she just waved, jumped behind the wheel, and without even waiting to look for any photographers in front of her car, sped off for her next destination. Word from the press who staked out her Brentwood home is that she arrived there about four.

"That's it from here, Christie. Back to you and Greg."

"Thanks, Lloyd."

"Just another night for the ultimate party animal."

"What a whirlwind of excitement."

"Nothing but energy, that girl."

"Nothing but fun."

"But you have to wonder if she'll ever work again."

"You have to wonder if she even cares."

"But she is awfully talented."

"No one denies it."

"But I guess when you're rich, beautiful, and twenty-three, you want to get all you can out of life."

"And there's no doubt that's what she's doing."

"And that's why we'll be following her to capture every heart-stopping moment."

"Can't let down her fans."

"Not a chance. Next, the latest lowdown on the tragic overdose and death of hip-hop star Poodle 15."

※ ※ ※

"We're back with more unbiased and impartial analysis. Mark Ledbetter, you were saying . . ."

"I can tell you exactly what they like about her. They know she speaks from the heart, so even if they disagree with her . . . well, they trust her."

"I don't know why they should disagree—"

"Marie Slocum—"

"She's speaking common sense conservatism—"

"While he's full of nothing but liberal gobbledy-gook—"

"Like this. These are Harrington's own words from his last interview with our own Tyler Williams on the subject of stem-cell research."

"On the one hand—"

"Yet we must also consider—"

"You have to understand the other side—"

"There are two legitimate points of view—"

"Yet I also wonder—"

"However—"

"I can see both sides of the argument—"

"Do you see what I mean? Now listen to Cassie McClellan on the some issue."

"I oppose all government-supported stem-cell research. Creating human life in order to destroy it recalls the worst actions of the Nazi regime."

"What about the possible medical benefits—"

"More liberal fantasy. I haven't seen any benefits, have you? There's no other side to this argument, no middle ground. Either you're responsible and moral, or you're not. And I am."

"That's the kind of straightforward talk Americans like."

"Does anybody think that such talk reinforces the popular notion that conservatives are anti-science, anti-education—"

"Oh, c'mon!"

"Don't be ridiculous!"

"Well, given the opposition to all discussion of climate change—"

"A ridiculous proposition if ever I've heard one—"

"Just another leftist scheme to suck money—"

"What a bunch of frauds—"

"And the undercurrent of opposition to the theory of evolution—"

"Must we really discuss this?"

"Not at all. Besides, it's time for a break. We'll be right back with *Report from the Right*."

※ ※ ※

"Good afternoon. We turn first to a news conference currently underway at police headquarters."

"— at one o'clock this morning."

"Where did you find him?"

"In an apartment on Southport Street and Lakewood Avenue."

"That's near the Berkeley Bordello, isn't it?"

"A couple of blocks away."

"Do you see any connection between the two cases?"

"Not so far."

"Was he alone when you arrested him?"

"Yes."

"Did he have the files with him?"

"He had some files, yes."

"Were they the ones taken from Dr. Lannahan's office?"

"We haven't had a chance to match up those that we found in Waldo Avery's possession with the ones that were reported as stolen, but it seems likely that they are the same ones, yes."

"Did he resist arrest?"

"He did not."

"What's his background?"

"He's a former army sergeant who has done a good deal of security work."

"Does he have a job?"

"He has no known employment."

"Did he explain why he stole the files?"

"No."

"Did he take anything else?"

"Not that we are aware."

"Did someone pay him to rob the doctor's office?"

"We are investigating that possibility."

"Did he mention anyone?"

"Not so far."

"When do you think you'll know?"

"That's hard to say."

"Do you think he's shielding someone?"

"We don't know."

"Do you have any additional suspects?"

"Not at this juncture. He seems to have carried out the robbery alone."

"Well, there you have it, Sue. An arrest has been made in the case of Dr. Lannahan's stolen psychiatric files."

※ ※ ※

"Jim, we have a new a bombshell about those patients' records stolen from the office of the eminent psychiatrist Dr. Simon Lannahan. Here's Cindy Howell."

"Sue, the police have examined those files, and as you might expect, they contain a lot of names. Some are famous, some not. But one name leaped out: Louise Parker Harrington, ex-wife of Senator Vance Harrington. Today the first Mrs. Harrington reluctantly met with the press."

"Yes, I have been his patient."

"For how long?"

"Almost two years."

"Why were you there?"

"Excuse me. I'm Mrs. Harrington's lawyer. And I have advised her not to answer any questions about her own medical condition."

"Does Senator Harrington know that you've been in therapy?"

"Of course."

"Is Dr. Lannahan the only therapist you've seen?"

"No, I've worked with two other doctors."

"Does the Senator know you've been seeing Dr. Lannahan?"

"I assume so."

"During that treatment, did you ever mention the Senator?"

"All the time. And why shouldn't I? Our relationship was one of the primary reasons I sought therapy."

"How often did you mention him?"

"Many, many times."

"Then his name would be in your file."

"Obviously."

"Please—"

"Did you ever say anything confidential about him?"

"I repeat: Mrs. Harrington will not answer anything further about the direction or substance of her own treatment."

"Would the Senator have any reason to be embarrassed by the contents of your file?"

"You'd have to ask him."

"What would you say?"

"I don't think he'd be pleased."

"If you didn't tell the Senator about your therapist, could he still have known that you were a patient of Dr. Lannahan?"

"I'm sure he did."

"How would he have found out?"

"My client cannot be expected to speculate upon such matters."

"Mrs. Harrington?"

"He works for the government, right? That means he has lots of methods at his disposal. I'm sure you're aware that Senators, Congressmen, and those in similar positions have countless ways to learn whatever they want to know."

"Do you think Senator Harrington used illegal means—"

"All I can say is that they regularly hire all sorts of people to do all sorts of unpleasant and illegal chores."

"When you were married to the Senator, were you aware of occasions when he hired such people?"

"Of course."

"Could you describe such an occasion?"

"I could, but I won't."

"As far as you know, did the Senator ever hire someone to break into an office?"

"He may have."

"Do you think he ordered the robbery of Dr. Lannahan's office?"

"I wouldn't be surprised."

"Why not?"

"He's in the middle of a campaign, isn't he? And under those circumstances, men in his position tend to become desperate, right?"

"Sue, the press conference went on a while longer, but here was the crucial moment. Whether Mrs. Harrington knew the effect of what she was saying is not clear, but there's no doubt that she laid down in front of the press the possibility . . . or maybe even the likelihood . . . that Senator Vance Harrington ordered a break-in at the office of psychiatrist Dr. Simon Lannahan in order to steal Mrs. Harrington's medical records and thereby protect himself from further accusations. Cindy Howell, *Channel 6 Action News.*"

"Thank you, Cindy."

"Well, Jim, you won't be surprised to learn that the McClellan campaign has scheduled a news conference one hour from now."

"And they're probably going to make these charges even plainer than Mrs. Harrington did."

"I'm sure they'll try."

"Can the Harrington campaign sustain another hit before election day?"

"They may have to."

"They're really piling up, aren't they?"

"I wonder if more will follow."

"I wouldn't be surprised."

"And we'll soon find out. Now here's sports."

▨ ▨ ▨

"Why doesn't he resign and save us all a lot of anguish?"

"Those were the words of Cassie McClellan, as she commented upon the latest revelations about Senator Vance Harrington. Here's Sue with more."

"Thanks, Jim. There was no venom in her voice, only sadness, as Congresswoman McClellan commented on the latest allegations against her opponent."

"I don't want to talk about this subject, but given the information released today, I have no choice."

"But you must have heard the Senator's press conference."

"I did. I listened and watched. And you know what struck me the hardest? That his wife didn't even appear . . . I'm talking about his present wife, not his former one . . . She didn't even stand by his side to show support. To my mind, that's an admission of guilt. She knows what he's done, and she's not going to tolerate it."

"But there's no proof he did anything wrong."

"Really? Look, I'm no lawyer, but the evidence is overwhelming. The resignation of Eileen Corbett, amid charges of infidelity. The testimony of Amber Stephens. All those text messages and e-mails. His name in the register of the . . . what do they call it? The Berkeley Bordello. Now the latest from the first Mrs. Harrington, who's obviously hiding a lot more than she cares to admit. How much more do we need?"

"His name was never mentioned—"

"Fine. You believe what you want. But I strongly suspect the voters are going to make their own feelings very clear on Election Day."

"What about—"

"No, that's enough. I'm finished talking about this ugly business."

"But what about—"

"I said forget it! I want to talk about the issues. The economy. Jobs. The deficit. The need to keep our military strong. Our struggle to protect the rights of the unborn and to preserve traditional marriage. These are my causes. And I'm not going to let myself or my campaign be distracted by this nonsense."

"And with that the Congresswoman left the stage."

"She really didn't answer questions, did she?"

"No, but she posed plenty of them, which are now swirling around Senator Harrington. And with just a little over a week to go, he doesn't have much time to clear them up. He probably wants to talk about other matters, but before he does, he'll have to deal with these charges."

"I had absolutely nothing to do with the break-in at the psychiatrist's office."

"Did you know your wife was a patient there?"

"Yes."

"Were you worried about what she might say?"

"Everything she's had to say has been out before the public for many years now."

"Then why do you suppose Dr. Lanahan's office was robbed?"

"I haven't the slightest idea."

"Do you blame the McClellan campaign?"

"I have no idea."

"Then you think they could be behind it."

"I have no idea what they're doing, except making outrageous accusations that lack even the slightest foundation in fact."

※ ※ ※

"Joe Lasher here, with another few hours of truth, justice, and the American way.

"I'm sure you're all glad to see that the liberals' favorite pin-up boy, Vance Harrington, is getting what he's long deserved. And of course, I'm only too pleased to help dish it out.

"In addition to the very convincing honey blonde Amber Stephens, we now have strong evidence that the Senator was not satisfied with just one or two women on the side. No, he needed a whole stable of girls, and he found them at the Berkeley Bordello.

"The only thing that's missing from this picture is the kinky stuff, but we should learn about that soon enough.

"How do I know? Well, I have a very reliable source that assures me that Vance Harrington's name has been discovered in the records of a nationwide porno ring.

"That's right. You heard me. Your man in Washington sits in front of his computer at night . . . or maybe during the day . . . looking for inspiration.

"Say, what do you figure he likes? Ropes? Whips? Chains?

"Or maybe his tastes are more exotic. Liberals are always promoting what they like to call 'alternative lifestyles.' Maybe Mr. Harrington likes his sex right-lefty. Or AC-DC.

"It's only a matter of time before we find out, folks. Sources tell me the story is ready to go 'Kaboom!' And when it does, guess who'll be right here to give you every delicious detail?

"Back in two minutes."

⊠ ⊠ ⊠

". . . in the name of our Lord, Amen."

"Amen."

"Doesn't it feel good to begin the day with a prayer?"

"It surely does, Reverend."

"Yes, it does. Now, however, I want to move to another subject, far more worldly, I'm afraid, but nonetheless one of great importance."

"I bet I know."

"I'm talking about the Senate race between one of our heroines, Cassie McClellan, and Vance Harrington."

"We've certainly been hearing a lot about him lately."

"But not everything is accurate."

"I'm not surprised. After all, he is a favorite of the liberal media."

"And they have a way of . . . well, let us say, playing with the truth."

"Don't we know it."

"That's why I'm so happy that our friends at home have been purchasing copies of our new documentary about Senator Harrington called *The Real Story*."

"I understand that sales have been terrific."

"They certainly have. But even so, I want to remind everyone that this new informative movie, which you can purchase on DVD for just $29.95, is vital to anyone who cares about the future of our country."

"It really hits the key issues, doesn't it?"

"Absolutely. For instance, we all know that Senator Harrington has been married once before. But how many people know that during his first marriage, he had a longstanding affair with a woman whose own first husband later died, supposedly of cancer."

"At least that's what they would have us believe."

"Exactly. Is that what happened? Or did he die under more mysterious circumstances?"

"We need to know. And the hospital refuses to release the autopsy."

"Meanwhile the police have closed the file."

"That's always a warning sign."

"The evidence keeps piling up, doesn't it?"

"It's unbelievable."

"And what about this . . . and I hate even to say the word . . . this brothel we keep hearing about?"

"The Berkeley Bordello?"

"Exactly. Why are authorities keeping Mr. Harrington's name out of the investigation? And how many of his friends are involved?"

"I'm very suspicious."

"And, Anne, do you remember that pro-life activist who died last year in a car accident?"

"Judd McClatchy?"

"What a brave man he was!"

"One of my personal heroes."

"And mine as well. Well, according to this documentary, his death may not have been an accident."

"What do you mean?"

"Some have suggested that he was the victim of foul play, killed by an underworld assassin."

"I hate to say this, but I would not be the slightest bit surprised."

"And if that's true, was Senator Harrington the one who planned the killing, then hired the killer?"

"Given what we know, that seems a distinct possibility."

"He wouldn't be the first."

"I've heard that he has many contacts on the wrong side of the law."

"Including a lot of people who have protected him over the years."

"And kept all his secrets."

"You mean about his reputed drug use."

"As well as his countless infidelities."

"And who knows how many women we're talking about?"

"Does this documentary, *The Real Story*, go into all that?"

"It does. And in great detail."

"Sounds like something everyone ought to see."

"And you know what else it uncovers?"

"What?"

"The truth about the break-in at the psychiatrist's office."

"Oh, my. I'm sure everyone's been waiting to learn about that!"

"Well, here's their chance to find out what the Senator and the President and an awful lot of people don't want us to learn."

"I'm so glad. Reverend, would you mind telling our viewers again how they can order this important DVD?"

"The same way they pay for everything, Anne. By check, by credit card, even sending us cash. I know a lot of companies don't accept cash, but we take everything."

"All they have to do is call or write. And the cost is $29.95."

"Plus tax and shipping."

"Of course. Can't get around the ol' federal tax."

"One day, Anne. One day."

"Hah-hah."

"So here's your chance to strike a blow against the atheistic, humanistic liberals who are trying to tear this country down."

"Let's do it to him before he does it to us."

"Amen."

▨ ▨ ▨

"Welcome back to *Capital Currents*. All right, ladies and gentlemen. It's prediction time. The moment when you have to put everything on the line. Let's start with the most controversial Senate race of all: Harrington vs. McClellan. Brock Cassidy?"

"I think McClellan's going to take it, Roy. The momentum is clearly on her side."

"One for McClellan. Flora O'Herlihy?"

"I cannot believe that the majority of the American public are foolish enough to fall for the palaver put out by the McClellan campaign. Harrington holds on."

"It's a tie ballgame. Nicole DiBoneventura?"

"Roy, women everywhere are fed up with Harrington's shenanigans. I think there's a feeling around the country that women are simply more honest, more dependable—"

"Is that what you think?"

"The evidence certainly leads us that way."

"Whose evidence?"

"Nicole, what's your prediction?"

"McClellan by three points, Roy. If not more."

"That makes it two to one. Neil Gosselin?"

"Harrington still has an unshakeable base, even under the onslaught of lies against him by the McClellan team."

"Who says they're lies?"

"And McClellan is too extreme for the vast majority of the American public—"

"What's extreme about her—"

"We still value fair play in this country—"

"We also value the truth—"

"And people know when a candidate is being slandered."

"She's aggressive, that's all."

"He has a record of achievement. She offers nothing but more antagonism."

"She offers traditional values—"

"Then, Neil, your vote is . . . ?

"Harrington in a squeaker."

"So it's two-to-two. And now it's up to me. I say . . . McClellan. By a nose!"

"It's Election Day, and the voting looks heavy.

"Good morning. I'm Jim Smathers."

"And I'm Sue Konstacky. Well, a long and bitter campaign reaches its climax today, as voters finally go to the polls and have their say. After all the vitriol and all the speeches, all the commentary and all the partisan attacks, the core of the democratic process is underway. One person, one vote.

"Lines are forming around the state, but locally they seem especially long. Here's Cindy Howell."

"Sue, I'm standing in the heart of what has traditionally been regarded as Harrington territory, the Mattesville suburbs, and if the Senator is watching, as we're sure he is, he ought to be very pleased.

"Here he is voting early this morning with his wife."

"How does it look, Senator?"

"We're feeling good."

"Are you expecting a high turnout?"

"That's what they say."

"You figure that's a good sign?"

"The more people that vote, the better for our side."

"It's supposed to rain this afternoon."

"Our side won't be discouraged. We've got the momentum."

"Sue, he certainly seemed to brim with confidence. Across town, though, at about the same time, Cassie and Phil McClellan cast their ballots, then took a few questions."

"How do things look, Congresswoman?"

"We're very hopeful."

"It's supposed to rain this afternoon."

"Is it? Well, our supporters are determined to make their presence felt, even in rough weather."

"May we ask who you voted for?"

"I think you know my answer."

"And you, Mr. McClellan?"

"I don't mind telling you that. I was very proud to vote for my wife. How many men can say that?"

"Congresswoman, what about the accusations—"

"See you later."

"And off they went."

"Cindy, it's Jim."

"Hi, Jim."

"The lines behind you seem to be moving slowly. Am I wrong? And is there an explanation?"

"It's hard to say. All we know is that some people have been waiting for over an hour outside, and, as one woman made very clear, tempers are beginning to fray."

"I have a job, y' know."

"How long have you been outside, ma'am?"

"Since seven o'clock. And I can't stay much longer."

"Any chance you'll skip voting this year?"

"No way. But they really ought to have more machines."

"Jim, she finally did get her chance to vote, but not until ten-oh-five. No one's saying anything official, but since this is Harrington territory, questions are being raised."

"Sue, we've now learned one reason why the lines at this particular polling center have been so long. It turns out that several machines in this area, which is part of Senator Harrington's home district, are malfunctioning."

"Cindy, when were these malfunctions noted?"

"About an hour ago."

"Have they been fixed?"

"We've been told that they have been. In fact, here's what Herman Kronkeit, a spokesman for the Board of Elections, said a little while ago."

"Two voting machines were inoperative for a part of the morning, but they have now been repaired, and I have every confidence that they will work efficiently for the rest of the day. We apologize for the inconvenience, and we expect that everyone who comes to vote will have the opportunity to do so."

"Can you guarantee that all votes cast earlier this morning have been counted accurately?"

"Not a single vote has been lost."

"What about the ones cast in the defective machines?"

"As soon as the machines went . . . awry, they stopped accepting votes. All votes previously cast were counted, and not one has been lost. Again, let me reassure everyone that all machines are now operational."

"Nonetheless, Jim, the lines remain long. Back to you."

"Cindy, in light of such delays, has anyone suggested keeping the polls open beyond the closing hour of eight o'clock?"

"Not so far, but if the number of voters continues at the present level, that possibility may be considered. Otherwise a great many citizens will be frustrated with the voting procedure, and the state might be vulnerable to lawsuits that could invalidate the entire process."

"Has anyone seriously proposed that idea?"

"I don't believe so, but I've heard rumblings among the voters themselves."

"They're not happy."

"That is definitely the case."

"We'll stay tuned, Cindy."

※ ※ ※

"The tightly competitive election between Senator Vance Harrington and the challenger, Congresswoman Cassie McClellan, remains intense, even on Election Day, when controversy continues to percolate. Here's Cindy Howell."

"Sue, we thought that all voting machines were repaired, but periodically today they have broken down."

"Are all running now?"

"For the moment. But the lines are still long, as people have been forced to wait for hours on this chilly November day."

"Given the length of those lines, will polls remain open later than normal?"

"We haven't heard anything, Jim ... I mean, Sue. But we may yet. Cindy Howell, *Channel 6 Action News*."

"Thanks, Cindy. Well, while all that was going on, another kind of voting controversy was brewing at a local college. Here's Ben Hansen."

"Jim, a lot of students at Masefield College, students whose home is in another city or state, have for a long time voted in our local elections. Well, today a lot of them were blocked from carrying out their civic duties. I spoke to one young woman who was turned away."

"What is your name?"

"Hannah Barrow."

"And what happened when you were waiting to vote?"

"Well, it was . . . like . . . the craziest thing."

"Could tell us what happened?"

"Sure . . . like, I was standing on line, waiting to . . . like . . . y'know, vote and everything, when this guy in a suit with . . . like . . . a badge or something comes over to me and . . . like, y'know . . . asks me for my identification and everything."

"Did he say who he was?"

"No. Like . . . no."

"What did you do?"

"Well . . . y'know, I showed him my I.D and everything. But he said that that wasn't . . . like . . . good enough."

"Then what happened?"

"He pulled me out of line, and said I . . . like . . . couldn't vote."

"Did he do that to anyone else?"

"Yeah. To like . . . a lot of kids."

"Who was he?"

"Nobody . . . like, y'know . . . knew. But he sure stopped a lotta people from like . . . voting."

"Is that man here now?"

"No, I haven't . . . like . . . seen him for a while."

"Was he removed?"

"Y'know . . . I don't know."

"Sue, after my conversation with Hannah, we learned that the man in question was a member of the local Conservative party, who had no authority whatsoever to prevent students from voting. In fact, he had no right to be anywhere near the voting machines. But somehow, and no one knows how, he managed to infiltrate the campus."

"Cindy, this is Jim."

"Hi, Jim."

"Any word of explanation from college officials?"

"They are nowhere to be found."

"Maybe they're voting downtown."

"Could be."

"But now all voting machines are open, and the paths are clear."

"So far. Even so, Sue . . . I mean, Jim—"

"This is Sue."

". . . we heard a lot of similar stories today, and I think we're in for a thorough investigation. No matter what the vote totals turn out to be tonight, this election may not be over for quite a while."

▨ ▨ ▨

"Good evening. The polls have just closed, and the votes are beginning to come in. I'm Jim Smathers."

"And I'm Sue Konstacky. Even as the numbers are tallied, questions abound concerning election irregularities. Here's Cindy Howell."

"Thanks, Sue and Jim. A couple of hour ago we reported about one polling station where delays were very long. Since then we've learned that others places were similarly victimized. Here's what one woman told me."

"We waited for hours to get inside. Then when we were finally there, only two machines were operating. For hundreds of people."

"Was the line moving slowly?"

"It hardly moved at all. You know who I feel sorry for?"

"Who's that?"

"Those people who had to wait for hours, then couldn't even get inside."

"And that seems to be the story, Jim. Several machines have broken down, all in densely populated districts that were supposed to be Harrington strongholds. No problems in the more rural areas, where Congresswoman Cassie McClellan was expected to draw her greatest strength. Back to you, Jim."

"Cindy, this is Sue."

"Yes, Sue?"

"Are you expecting the Harrington side to take legal action?"

"Well, first we'll have to see the results—"

"Of course, but if Harrington falls short—"

"As would seem to be a distinct possibility, if early exit polls are any indication of voter trends—"

"Of course, if Harrington wins—"

"I'm sorry, I couldn't hear you—"

"I was saying that if Harrington wins, what's to stop the McClellan forces from lodging a protest of their own—"

"Nothing at all, Sue."

"Cindy, this is Jim. We also have to keep in mind there were the controversies at several colleges—"

"Right again, Jim. And they were supposed to be another source of strong Harrington support."

"In other words, a lot of issues remain unsettled."

"That is exactly the case."

"Cindy, this is Sue."

"Yes, Jim?"

"No, Sue."

"Sorry! Go ahead."

"To your knowledge, have any polling stations remained open beyond the appointed hour?"

"Not that I'm aware of."

"In that case, was anyone left literally out in the cold?"

"Again, there might have been a few, but at this point we can't say for sure."

"I suppose the big question is how many potential voters saw the massive crowds and didn't bother waiting, but simply turned around and went home."

"We'll find out soon enough, Jim."

"This is Sue. Stay on the story, Cindy. We'll be back to you soon."

"Thanks."

"Now let's check the numbers."

"Only 3% have reported, and Harrington holds a slight lead."

"Any trends so far?"

"Nothing I can see."

"We'll keep an eye on it. Now let's move to some local races."

"Where we are looking at an upset in the race for Moon Bay Comptroller."

⊠ ⊠ ⊠

"Sue, the excitement is building here."

"Go ahead, Cindy."

"The crowd is energized. They feel that victory is within their grasp. And they're threatening to raise the roof."

"Any word from the candidate?"

"Not so far, but with the vote this close, we're not expecting any official word for some time."

"Well, Cindy, with 50% of the vote counted, the candidates are separated by a mere 1,375 votes."

"Which is less than 1%. But with each new set of numbers, and as the gap continues to narrow, even that small difference is enough to send supporters of Congresswoman Cassie McClellan into screams of joy."

"Meanwhile, at Harrington Headquarters, the mood is beginning to pick up, as their man cuts into what was once a substantial McClellan lead. Here's Ben Hansen."

"Jim, that certainly seems to be the case. Earlier tonight, when the first results were tallied, supporters of Senator Harrington feared the worst. But as the evening has worn on, and the numbers tilt Harrington's way, the cheers and the celebrations are spreading. I spoke to one campaign spokesman, Alexander Felton, just a few minutes ago."

"Alex, you must be relieved at the way matters are proceding."

"You could say that. Every trend is positive, and we're confident that by the time all the votes are tallied, we'll be on top by a comfortable margin."

"But will all the votes be counted?"

"Are you talking about the machines that broke down?"

"Among other problems."

"Let's put it this way. The other side may have tried to sabotage this election, but despite their antics, we're still confident."

"Are you accusing the McClellan team of conspiracy?"

"I'm not making any accusations, but we've certainly heard rumors, and we have no reason to doubt them."

"What about the lost student votes?"

"Once again, McClellan people were armed with phony IDs and placed strategically to prevent these young people from carrying out their constitutional right."

"Do you plan to take any action?"

"Once the election is over, and we're back in office, we'll conduct a thorough investigation. The American people have a right to know what Ms. McClellan and her team tried to pull."

"You sound confident you're going to win."

"I know we will."

"Sue, you heard him. The Harrington team feels good."

"It's Jim, Ben. We'll be back to you."

"Okay!"

"Well, Felton seemed pretty confident."

"Although his man is still behind."

"Right. Let's check the board. Bruce?"

"Thanks, Sue. Well, as everyone can see, with 53% of the vote counted, it's 49% for McClellan, 48% for Harrington, and the rest scattered among several minor party candidates."

"Assuming those numbers remain the same, what's the likelihood of a recount?"

"If the two candidates end up separated by less than 1%, we go to recount. That's state law."

"And that would also leave time to clear up all charges of voter fraud."

"Along with everything else that's gone down tonight."

"Thanks, Bruce. Well, ladies and gentlemen, one thing is clear: if this race hasn't brought us enough drama so far, we may be in for one of the most fascinating electoral stories of our time."

▨ ▨ ▨

"Bruce, tell us about the Board."

"Jim, we have 99% of the votes tallied, and it couldn't be closer. Both candidates have 49% of the vote, with McClellan ahead by a bare 456 votes."

"That's according to the most totals."

"Absolutely."

"In other words, it's recount time."

"It looks inevitable."

"Then let's fasten our seat belts because— Wait a minute, we're going to McClellan headquarters. Here's Cindy Howell."

"Thanks, Sue. I can barely hear you over the shouting as Congress-woman McClellan, with her family in tow, makes her way to the micro-phone. Here she goes."

"Thank you! Thank you!"

"Yay!"

"Well, it's been another great night, hasn't it?"

'YAY!"

"They tell me the numbers are close, but there's no doubt about it! We're winning!"

"Yay!"

"It was tight, but we pulled it out!"

"Yay!"

"Thanks to you, thanks to a wonderful team, thanks to my family, and thanks to God!"

"YAY!"

"I know what the networks are saying—"

"Boooooooooooooooooo!"

"Right! How much can we trust them?"

"Hah-hah!"

"But there does seem to be the possibility of a recount."

"Boooooooooooooooooo!"

"Yup, that's the way it looks. Unless, of course, Senator Harrington does the gentlemanly thing and gets out now. Before he suffers any more humiliation!"

"YAY!"

"Instead, it looks like he's going to try to stir up as much trouble as he can—"

"Boooooooooooooooooo!"

"Blaming us for problems we had nothing to do with. Doing any-thing to try to somehow salvage a race he has clearly lost!"

※ ※ ※

"This race is far from over!"

"Yay!"

"That was Senator Vance Harrington last night, addressing a crowd of supporters after the final vote totals were announced."

"Good afternoon, I'm Jim Smathers.

"'Never-say-die' was the spirit last night, as Senator Harrington tried to rally his forces, who were clearly dispirited after finding their candidate behind by even so small a margin. Here's more from the Senator."

"The other side has used despicable tactics against us. They've lied, and they've bribed, and they've stolen, and they've pulled enough dirty tricks for five elections.

"But we're standing tall, we're going to have all the charges investigated, and at the end of the day I can promise you one thing: we're going to win!"

"Yay!"

"Don't give up hope!"

"If the response last night was any indication, some of the Senator's supporters clearly have surrendered hope. Here's Ben Hansen."

"Jim, this race was originally supposed to be a runaway for Senator Harrington, a 'last hurrah,' if you will. But he and his team never figured on the campaign skills of Congresswoman McClellan."

"Ben—"

"And they certainly never expected the onslaught of ugly attacks that simply proved too much of a distraction for the voters."

"Ben, what about the matter of defective machines and the questions over voter registration and participation?"

"There's a lot of controversy out there, Jim. The question, how much can be investigated in a very short time frame? Ben Hansen, *Channel 6 Action News*."

"The Board of Elections has announced that the recount will begin as soon as possible. Meanwhile the Harrington campaign has taken steps to postpone this recount while other charges can be studied, but there's no telling how the State Supreme Court will rule."

▨ ▨ ▨

"New numbers as the Senate election tightens."

"Good afternoon. I'm Sue Konstacky. As the recount continues state-wide, the tally in the race for U.S. Senator has grown even closer. Here's Cindy Howell."

"Sue, if you can believe it, with the recount about halfway through, the margin between Senator Vance Harrington and Congresswoman Cassie McClellan is now down to a mere forty-three votes. Some irregularities were found in machines from Pelton County, and newly discovered votes there have brought Senator Harrington to almost a literal tie with his challenger."

"Any word from the Senator?"

"Nothing official, but a spokesman for his team expressed confidence that the continued investigation would soon lead to a Harrington victory by the end of the week."

"And how about the McClellan campaign?"

"Again, nothing official, but a spokeswoman noted that 'the Congress-woman is still ahead.' They don't seem worried. Back to you, Sue."

"Thanks, Cindy. Well, you may remember that on Election Day we reported how at several colleges, students were pulled out of voting lines and required to provide extra identification. This morning one of those fake election officials was arrested. His name is Albert Costello, and he apparently works for the State Conservative Party. Officials tell us he's said little thus far, but they expect to have more information soon.

"Now here's Tim with the weather."

⸙ ⸙ ⸙

"Harrington takes the lead!"

"Good afternoon. This is Sue Konstacky. Let's jump right to our top story.

"With the recount in the race for United States Senator nearing its end, for the first time Senator Vance Harrington has opened a gap of nearly three hundred votes. Here's Cindy Howell."

"Thanks, Sue. Today the Harrington campaign expressed confidence that they would triumph in this incredibly close selection. Here's spokes-woman Ellen Marlborough."

"We believe that we're finally learning the accurate totals of the votes cast on Election Day. We're also hopeful that as more irregularities are corrected, the margin of victory will grow."

"Sue, they're feeling good. No doubt about it. Cindy Howell, *Channel 6 Action News.*"

"Thanks, Cindy. In a related story, we've learned that Albert Costello, recently arrested as part of a team of conservative activists accused of harassing young voters, has admitted that he was hired by leaders of the local Conservative Party to, in his words, "validate" the recent electoral process. When asked whether he was recruited specifically by the McClellan campaign, Costello denied any connection with that organization.
"Today our Ben Hansen spoke with Frederick Thielman, local Conservative leader."

"Mr. Thielman, what's your response to these charges?"
"I am unaware that anyone in our organization paid Mr. Costello for any services rendered."
"But he claims—"
"What we do know is that in past elections, many students voted illegally. Mr. Costello may simply have taken it upon himself to try to remedy that situation."
"But you disclaim any connection—"
"I've never met the man. Or if I have, I don't remember him."
"Then why—"
"Apparently he was motivated by a patriotic fervor that went out of control."

"And that's where the story stands. Back to you, Sue."
"Thanks, Ben. Keep on that story."
"I definitely will."
"Now here's Herbie with sports."

✖ ✖ ✖

"And the margin grows!

"Good afternoon. I'm Sue Konstacky. New tallies in the recount for the election for United States Senator show that the incumbent, Senator Vance Harrington, is now ahead by nearly 2,000 votes. Here's Cindy Howell."

"Thank, Sue. Well, the Harrington campaign could barely contain its joy today, as their lead over Congresswoman Cassie McClellan grew to what seems like an overwhelming 1,962 votes. Here's Harrington spokeswoman Ellen Marlborough."

"The new numbers are certainly gratifying, but we've always been confident that the election would go our way. We trusted in the wisdom of the voters, and they have justified that faith. Now we look forward to working with Senator Harrington to serve the people of our state and the country."

"Meanwhile, the McClellan campaign was not surrendering."

"There's a long way to go. We admit that at this moment things are not looking bright, but with faith in God, we believe that Congresswoman McClellan will emerge triumphant."

"Sue, that's what they say, but the outlook for the McClellan campaign is grim. Cindy Howell, *Channel 6 Action News.*"

▦ ▦ ▦

"And we have a winner!"
"Good afternoon. I'm Sue Konstacky.
"One of the closest Senate elections in American history has finally ended. Here with details is Cindy Howell."

"Sue, the crucial moment came last week when, in a stunning reversal, the State Board of Elections nullified almost 3,900 votes originally tallied for Senator Vance Harrington. Apparently they were recorded twice by defective machines that mistakenly added those votes to Harrington's total. The result is that the recount has ended, the Secretary of State has certified Congresswoman Cassie McClellan as the winner, and our state has a new Senator.

"Here's her reaction this morning."

"Well, it's been a long struggle, but we've done it!"

"Yay!"

"We fought against the entrenched left-wing political powers, as well as all their fellow travelers in the media, and we finally won!"

"Yay!"

"They thought they had us, and I have to admit . . . things looked a little shaky a week ago!"

"Hah-hah!"

"But our reliance on God and our faith in the American political system has sustained us. Now it's off to carry our message and our values to Washington!"

"YAY!"

"Lower taxes!"

"Yay!"

"Less wasteful spending!"

"Yay!"

"Less governmental interference!"

"Yay!"

"Respect for the power of prayer and respect for all human life, no matter young and helpless!"

"In other words, the restoration of good ol' traditional American values!"

"YAY!"

"Thank you to everyone for your love and your support and your prayers."

"YAY!"

"Now let's take back our country!"

"It's hard to imagine a more joyous scene, Sue."

"Indeed. Cindy, any word from the Harrington campaign?"

"Nothing official so far. Although I have heard reports that they will not accept this verdict passively. They remain convinced that the election was crooked, and they are equally positive that conservative elements throughout the state conspired against them. Thus we can definitely expect more legal challenges on their part."

"Then Senator Harrington has not conceded the race."

"He absolutely has not."

※ ※ ※

"We're sitting with Senator Vance Harrington. Sir, thank you for your time."

"Good to be with you."

"Let me ask first if you've formally conceded the election to Cassie McClellan."

"I have not."

"Do you ever intend to do so?"

"I have no plans in that direction."

"Then let me ask you point blank: do you believe this election was fairly decided?"

"I do not."

"Would you say it was in fact stolen?"

"I'm sorry to speak in such harsh terms, but yes, I believe it was."

"Do you have any more legal alternatives available?"

"We are looking into all sorts of possibilities."

"Yet the election has been certified—"

"I know—"

"And in several weeks Ms. McClellan will be sworn in—"

"I know that, too—"

"So it would seem that your options have run out."

"Unless our investigations yield new information."

"What kind of information?"

"We'll know it when we find it."

"Do you believe that revelations are out there?"

"I have every confidence that they are."

"In the meantime, any words to Ms. McClellan?"

"She knows my feelings."

"Do you believe that the personal attacks on your character were orchestrated by her campaign?"

"I do."

"Is that part of what you hope to uncover?"

"I don't want to reveal too much."

"But that's what you're looking for."

"Among other matters."

"Any words about the future of our country? Any words to comfort your loyal supporters?"

"Let's just say that Ms. McClellan's vision of America is not mine, and I hope that my party will oppose her and her ilk at every turn. If her values ever become the law of the land, this country will be in serious trouble."

"That's not a very positive note on which to end your many years of government service."

"I suppose not. So let me add this: every once in a while a few men and woman march into Washington under a strict conservative banner, but they surprise us by turning out to be decent people. Let's hope that Ms. McClellan is one of those rare ones."

The Aftermath

"I firmly support the Governor's proposed preventive measures."

"Good evening, and welcome to *Channel 6 Action News*. I'm Jim Smathers.

"That was newly elected Senator Cassie McClellan offering her endorsement of new guidelines for women's health clinics. These strictures include the number of square feet for recovery rooms, the temperature of those rooms, the reading materials distributed to patients, including anti-abortion fliers, and hours the clinics may be in service. Here's more of what Senator McClellan said."

"We want to do everything possible to protect women, and we want to provide them with the most medically safe environment possible."

"Opponents of these measures, however, saw such regulations as an attempt to curtail the services provided."

"These supposed 'guidelines' are nothing more than a back-handed ploy to undermine the rights of women to have all procedures available, including abortion. That Senator McClellan has chosen to deny women these resources fulfills our worst fears about her."

"The legality of these measures is currently before the State Court of Appeals, and observers predict it will be some time before the case is resolved.

"In other action, Senator McClellan further angered opponents by blocking a vote on the confirmation of a judge for that court. Judge Natalie Potter was given the highest rate by the American Bar Association, and was actually endorsed by Senator McClellan's predecessor, Vance Harrington, but today Senator McClellan spoke against many of the Judge's rulings."

"In her time as a judge, Judge Potter has been an activist who legislates from the bench. I cannot support someone whose vision so sharply contradicts my own. A judge should interpret the Constitution, not rewrite it."

"A prolonged battle over this nomination is expected. We'll be right back."

❖ ❖ ❖

"Welcome back. This is Jim Smathers. Sue Konstacky is on assignment.

"Well, post-election investigations have gone on for two weeks, and the results are finally in. Here's Cindy Howell."

"Jim, the election was fair. At least that's what the State Board of Elections claims. They say the votes were counted accurately, and that Cassie McClellan is a legitimate member of the United States Senate. Chairman Herman Kronkeit made the announcement."

"Our inquiry took two directions.

"One, we checked whether all voting machines tallied votes accurately. We have concluded that except for a few minutes in the morning, the machines were indeed working to our expectations."

"Sir, did you—"

"I'll take questions in a minute."

"Sir—"

"In a minute! We also determined that only a very small number of students were pulled out of the voting lines, and virtually all had an opportunity to vote later that day."

"Sir—"

"In other words, the results of the Senatorial contest were certified properly. Now I'll take questions."

"Sir, did you ascertain whether a sufficient number of voting machines were available in all districts, particularly those that were expected to go strongly for Harrington?"

"That matter was not within our jurisdiction."

"Why not?"

"We were assigned only to confirm that those machines in use functioned properly."

"Then you can't say that a sufficient number were brought in."

"We don't know."

"But—"

"As I explained, the matter was not within our jurisdiction."

"Then the question still remains."

"In your mind, perhaps. Not in ours."

"Have you spoken to all students who were pulled out of the line?"

"We could not find them all."

"Then how do you know that they had a chance to vote later?"

"We have based our judgment on a representative sample."

"So you might have missed hundreds or even thousands from across the state."

"We are convinced that our conclusion is accurate."

"Jim, Mr. Kronkeit was insistent that his agency had completed its assignment properly. I'm not sure that everyone on the Harrington side will be satisfied, but all indications suggest that they have no recourse but to accept them."

⌧ ⌧ ⌧

"Finally, a few words about the wrap-up to one of the closest Senate elections in this country's history. Brock Cassidy?"

"Roy, liberals may hate her even more, but the evidence confirms that Cassie McClellan is going to do exactly as she promised: govern as a strict conservative."

"Flora O'Herlihy?"

"Questions of legitimacy still remain, and I suppose they always will—"

"Only for you—"

"But the Vance Harrington team is apparently out of options. All I can say is that I'm dreading a grim six years."

"Neil Gosselin?"

"She's already proven herself to be a nightmare. I hate to think what will happen when she actually begins to obtain power."

"Nicole DiBoneventura?"

"It's called democracy in action, Neil. And now she has a chance to help enact legislation that will benefit us all."

"Why is it that when liberals put their ideas into action—"

"Flora?"

"Conservatives claim that bills are being shoved down their throats, but when conservatives push through calamitous laws, it's democracy in action?"

"No one ever said that—"

"Conservatives say it all the time—"

"No, we don't—"

"Any law they don't like—"

"Let's grow up, people—"

"And I still say her whole campaign stinks—"

"Sore losers as always—"

"You had your commission—"

"Run by conservatives—"

"A commission's a commission—"

"There are still plenty of questions—"

"Time to move on—"

"For the moment—"

"I'm telling you. The tactics of the McClellan campaign will come back to haunt them."

"Dream on."

※ ※ ※

"Back to local news. Jim?"

"Thanks, Sue. Well, here's a name we haven't heard for a while: Waldo Avery. Sound familiar? He's the fellow who was convicted of breaking into the office of the eminent psychiatrist Dr. Simon Lannahan. That's where Avery stole a bunch of files, including that of the wife of former Senator Vance Harrington.

"Until now, everyone has always assumed that Avery, a decorated Army veteran, was conducting a one-man rogue operation, but today authorities have learned that he was actually in the employ of someone else. Here's Cindy Howell."

"Right you are, Jim. And that someone else is none other than L. Meredith Burnham, the reclusive newspaper tycoon who has financed a stream of arch-conservative political candidates and causes from all across the country. Here's what Police Chief Ryan Galsworthy had to say."

"Mr. Avery was paid by Mr. Burnham's organization not only to break into this particular office, but also to conduct a series of sabotage operations against liberal candidates from Washington to Florida. We are continuing our investigation, in conjunction with Departments from other states, and will provide details as they emerge."

"Jim, these revelations are explosive, to say the least."

"Indeed they are. Any word on when we'll learn more?"

"We expect further information later this week."

"We'll be waiting.

"Meanwhile, a spokeswoman for the Crandall Corporation announced today that despite contracts signed last fall, further layoffs would take place at the end of the month. Here's Ben Hansen."

"Jim, this one took a lot of people by surprise. Here are the words of spokeswoman Eleanor Cabot."

"The Crandall Corporation regrets that because of rising costs and expenses, the company is forced to make further cuts in personnel."

"But the reaction from workers was hardly so serene."

"They've broken their word!"

"They promised no more cuts!"

"We gave into them, and we believed them!"

"They lied to us!"

"Jim, right now union tempers are very short. And although most of the anger is directed against the Crandall Corporation, a portion is also aimed at Senator Cassie McClellan, who gained office partly on what she claimed was a settlement with Crandall to keep all these jobs that were just eliminated. Here's what one plant worker told us."

"It was only a few months ago that she said she had it all worked out. She even said her husband had surrendered his job for our cause. That's why we believed her, and that's why we voted for her!"

"Do you blame her for your losing these jobs?"

"She said the company would be set for years!"

"Conditions do change, of course—"

"Forget conditions! We trusted her, and she went back on her word!"

"Maybe the company had no choice."

"They had a choice! Anyway, where is she now? That's what I want to know."

"She's in Washington."

"Living it up with her fat cat friends!"

"Do you regret voting for her?"

"Are you kidding? One thing about unions, fella. They have a very long memory. We remember who stood with us, and who remember who betrayed us. And Cassie McClellan just kicked us in the teeth!"

"Jim, the Senator should consider herself lucky that she has five more years to win back these voters. Ben Hansen, *Channel 6 Action News*."

◼ ◼ ◼

"I'm Sue Konstacky, and our lead story tonight contains more details about the Senate campaign that apparently just won't end. Here's Cindy Howell."

"Sue, calls are coming from far and wide for Senator Cassie McClellan to explain the extent of her relationship with mysterious billionaire L. Meredith Burnham. Here's what Congressman Martin Suggs said today."

"First we learned that Burnham paid Waldo Avery to burglarize Dr. Lannahan's office and to confiscate confidential materials that subsequently worked in favor of the McClellan campaign.

"Next we discovered that among the Burnham donations that he gave to Conservative organizations is more than 1.2 million that ended up in the coffers of . . . you guessed it: the McClellan campaign.

"That's why we demand to know, first, whether Waldo Avery was actually a member of the McClellan organization, and, second, whether he carried out his crimes with the full knowledge and support of the candidate, her husband, and her team. If such is the case, we want to know what other services, legal or illegal, he provided.

"Furthermore, if laws have been broken, and the evidence is overwhelming that they have, we call on the Senator to answer these charges in court."

"Sue, this is getting nasty. Senator McClellan's victory may still be technically clear, but suddenly it seems tainted. Cindy Howell, *Channel 6 Action News*."

"Thanks, Cindy. We move directly to Washington, where Ralph Fears brings us a statement from the McClellan team."

"Senator McClellan took time out today to meet with reporters."

"Let me state categorically that I have never met or spoken to Waldo Avery. Furthermore, at no time did I authorize my campaign to pay him anything. To the best of my understanding, he operates with no official sanction, and therefore I disclaim all responsibility for his actions."

"I do know Mr. L. Meredith Burnham, and I am aware that some donations he made to various patriotic organizations were turned over to our team. All these contributions have been reported to the proper authorities and in appropriate form.

"Thank you, ladies and gentlemen."

"Senator McClellan tried to end the session there, but reporters were persistent."

"You said you never talked to Avery—"
"I said I've never met him."
"But did any member of your staff meet with him?"
"I'm not responsible for the actions of my staff."
"But if they did meet with him—"
"I was not present at any meeting."
"But are you aware of any—"

"Look, I have important matters to consider. I have no intention of playing the media game of 'gotcha' and replaying a campaign decided long ago."

"Did you ever speak to Mr. Burnham?"

"I already said that I have done so."

"Did he ever mention Avery?"

"I don't recall any references to anyone named Avery."

"Did he mention a specific sum of money that would be given to you?"

"We did not talk about money. We enjoyed a frank discussion of the issues, and I recall his saying that he was pleased with my views and would be happy to support my candidacy."

"Did that include breaking and entering—"

"I've already answered that. Thank you."

"Have you met with workers at the Crandall Corporation?"

"Not yet. But I intend to."

"How do you feel about the anger directed against you?"

"My husband and I both feel hurt. Apparently the management of the company has reneged on the deal we arranged, and I intend to get to the bottom of the situation."

"Will you—"

"Thank you."

"And that's where it ended. Clearly Senator McClellan hopes that this Avery story will fade away. But the winds of scandal are stirring, and in Washington such breezes rarely blow kindly. This is Ralph Favors reporting from the Senate."

※ ※ ※

"Finally, panel, we turn to the election that will not die, as new questions surround the victory by Cassie McClellan. Do they amount to anything more than a petty annoyance? Brock Cassidy?"

"Roy, this is the proverbial tempest in a teapot. A lot of fuss about very little—"

"She's going to have problems—"

"Flora O'Herlihy?"

"Mark my words. All her sleaze is going to come back to—"

"Oh, please!"

"Nicole DiBoneventura, you wanted to say—"

"This is so clearly a desperate attempt by a washed-up former officeholder to undermine the—"

"You mean Vance Harrington—"

"He has nothing to back up any of his ridiculous allegations. And everybody knows he has nothing—"

"There's more here, trust me—"

"Neil Gosselin—"

"There's a lot more. And she's going to have a hard time escaping the spotlight on this one—"

"She took a little money—"

"She knows a lot more about it—"

"Even if she does—"

"A lot more—"

"That doesn't make anything she did criminal—"

"But we haven't heard all that she did—"

"Because she didn't do anything—"

"She did plenty—"

"Is there evidence—"

"There will be—

"She has nothing to worry about—"

"She'll have plenty to worry about—"

"Unless some startling revelations are brought out—"

"Wait for 'em—"

"What could they be?"

"Just wait."

"And that's what we'll have to do until next week. This has been *Capital Currents*."

⊠ ⊠ ⊠

"The unhappiness at the Crandall Corporation is turning into a raging storm, as unions all over the state have joined their brothers and sisters in solidarity.

"Good evening. I'm Jim Smathers, and this is *Channel 6 Action News*.

"Labor is in an uproar, as recent firings by Crandall have infuriated workers everywhere. In the meantime, marches and protests are planned for the upcoming weeks. Here with a report is Cindy Howell."

"Jim, it's not just the firings themselves that have inspired this fury. Rather it is Crandall Corporation's calculated disregard for their own words. Here are samples of what we heard today."

"Why did they promise us?"
"Was it just to keep us quiet so they could win the election?"
"They knew what they were doing the whole time!"
"Bunch of liars! That's all they are! Bunch of liars!"
"And Cassie McClellan is the worst!"

"Jim, that last sentiment has resonated with everyone to whom we spoke. Maybe at this moment some political figure somewhere is more unpopular with the unions than Senator Cassie McClellan, but I'm not sure who that person might be.

"When a strike was threatened during the campaign, she seemed to reverse her longstanding policies and stand with the unions. Her husband even quit his job in support of the workers.

"Well, now it's only a few short months later, and more workers have been let go. Meanwhile the promises made by Cassie McClellan sound awfully hollow. Cindy Howell, *Channel 6 Action News*."

"Thanks, Cindy. In what is probably an unrelated story, another voice from the election just past has surfaced again. Her name is Amber Stephens, and you'll remember her as the honey blonde former staff member for Senator Vance Harrington who claimed that she had had an affair with him. You may also remember that during the closing days of the election, police uncovered a call girl service operating right here in town. Well, it turns out that those two stories are not unrelated. Here's Ben Hansen."

"Thanks, Jim. Well, here's what we knew before today. Amber Stephens worked for Senator Harrington, then was fired. Meanwhile the so-called Berkeley Bordello on Madison and Lakewood had operated for years.

"Well, today we learned of a connection. After Amber Stephens left Harrington's employ, she went to work at the Bordello, where she was often paid thousands of dollars to provide what have been called 'services' for some of the wealthiest business executives, politicians, sports and entertainment stars, and other prominent men from across the country. This is what her lawyer had to say."

"We are outraged that Ms. Stephens's name has been released from a book that was supposed to be kept confidential. Nonetheless, we admit that after she was fired by Senator Harrington, she needed to earn money, and in desperation accepted employment at the Berkeley. She is not proud of her record, but she had to survive."

"A slew of questions followed."

"Does Ms. Stephens still insist that she and the Senator had an affair?"
"Yes, I do."
"Are you sure? The Senator has always insisted that you misunderstood his intentions."
"I loved him, and he rejected me."
"Did he ever say that he loved you?"
"I felt that he cared for me a lot."
"Did he say that he did?"
"Maybe not in those exact words."
"What words did he use?"
"I don't remember. I just know that he cared for me. I could feel it by the way he looked at me."
"How did he look at you?"
"As if he loved me."

"Jim, the questions then turned to the time after she was fired."

"Did you ever see the Senator at the Berkeley?"
"No."
"Did you hear his name mentioned when you were there?"
"No."

"Jim, you'll recall that during the campaign, the McClellan campaign insisted that Senator Harrington's name was found in the ledger of the Berkeley as one of their clients. Today Ms. Stephens seemed to deny that assertion."

"After you were fired, did you ever see Senator Harrington again?"
"No."
"Did you—"
"Except on television."
"But never at the Berkeley."
"No."
"During the election campaign, you said you had lots of pictures and e-mails. Do you still have them?"
"Some."
"Do you plan to release any of them to the public?"
"I . . . I don't know!"
"When will you decide?"
"I DON'T KNOW!"

"Jim, with that pathetic cry, Ms. Stephens hurried away, shielded from further questions by her lawyer.

"She didn't absolve Vance Harrington of the charges she made earlier, but it certainly looks like a lot people jumped the gun in believing all the rumors put forward about the former Senator."

"Ben, a lot of those claims were put out by the McClellan campaign team."

"Right you are, Jim."
"Any word from them about this latest bulletin?"
"Not so far."
"Then they haven't admitted that they made mistakes."
"They have not."
"If indeed they were mistakes."
"Exactly, Jim. The question now looming is whether Senator Cassie McClellan campaign team deliberated published lies about Amber Stephens and the Berkeley Bordello in order to smear their opponent, former Senator Vance Harrington. And if it is ever confirmed that they did so, what will be the ramifications?"

"The story gets wilder every day."

"Unbelievable."

"But whatever happens, there's nothing anyone can do about the Senate race, is there? I mean, it's over, right?"

"At this point it is, but I wouldn't want to hazard a guess. It's simply impossible to gauge the next twist or turn. But everyone is definitely waiting."

"And so are we. Thanks, Ben."

⬚ ⬚ ⬚

"—interrupt this program with a news bulletin."

"Good afternoon. I'm Jim Smathers, and we're going right now to the U.S. District Court Office, where some shocking news is being presented by the District Attorney."

"—information has just been released about the names found in the register of the so-called 'Berkeley Bordello.' Among those on that list was Philip McClellan, former labor negotiator at the Crandall Corporation and the husband of U.S. Senator Cassie McClellan. Apparently Mr. McClellan was a regular client."

"Do you have any idea he went there?"

"At least several times."

"Can you tell us if he saw one special woman?"

"I can't say."

"Does the book indicate how much he paid each time he visited?"

"Overall, we're talking about tens of thousands of dollars."

"And there were quite a few visits."

"Quite a few."

"Jim, this is Ben."

"Go ahead, Ben."

"To say that this news is stunning is an understatement, to say the least."

"It's unbelievable. Any word yet from the McClellan team?"

"Nothing so far."

"Are we expecting a statement?"

"We are, although it's hard to imagine what they can say. The evidence is right there in black and white."

"Why has this material been released now?"

"Again, we don't know. Maybe someone was eager to take revenge against the Senator. In any case, the book in question must have been appropriated from the police department, or maybe a copy was stolen from the District Attorney's office. Or maybe there's some other reason. There's no telling what happened."

"All we know for sure is that this news is a bombshell."

"It certainly is."

"Thanks, Ben. To repeat: the name 'Philip McClellan,' husband of newly elected United States Senator Cassie McClellan, has been discovered in the list of clients in the books of the notorious 'Berkeley Bordello.'

"As soon as we learn more information, we'll be back."

▨ ▨ ▨

"The report that Philip McClellan, husband of Senator Cassie McClellan, was a regular client at the 'Berkeley Bordello' has finally brought a response from the Senator. Here she is speaking today on Capital Hill."

"I have spoken to my husband, and he explained to me that over the past few years he occasionally visited the establishment in question. He explained the circumstances of these visits, and he has asked me to forgive him. Without delving into our personal conversations, I shall say simply that I have done so.

"We intend to remain together as a couple, both for our children and for ourselves. We both believe that our marriage is strong enough to survive even this painful episode, which will not interfere with my performing the duties of my office. Thank you."

"Why isn't your husband here with you?"

"He wanted me to speak for both of us."

"Will he ever answer questions?"

"That's up to him."

"Did he tell you how many times he went there?"

"He told me that he visited the establishment on at least a dozen occasions."

"At least a dozen?"

"Approximately a dozen."

"You mentioned that you two discussed the 'circumstances' of his visits. Exactly what 'circumstances' did you discuss?"

"I prefer not to go into detail."

"Did your husband give you any reasons why he went?"

"As I said, I shall not discuss our private conversations."

"Was he jealous of your success?"

"I don't believe so."

"Did he ever say he felt threatened?"

"Don't be ridiculous."

"When was the last time he went there?"

"Several months ago."

"Before this latest report, did you know that he was a client there?"

"I was aware, yes."

"When did you learn the truth?"

"Roughly six months ago."

"Before or after his last visit?"

"After."

"Did you consider dropping out of the campaign?"

"I did, but our cause is more important than I am."

"During the campaign, you hinted very strongly that you believed Senator Vance Harrington was also a client there."

"I merely reacted to what I heard—"

"Yet his name has not been found in the book. Do you regret implicating him in the story?"

"You mean, his name hasn't been found *yet*."

"Do you believe it will be?"

"I don't know. I'm not thinking about Mr. Harrington right now."

"Will you and your husband ever appear together to answer questions about this matter?"

"We shall not. In fact, this is the last time I expect to address the issue."

"But will he ever speak to us—"

"That's all, ladies and gentlemen."

"When can we expect a statement from him—"

"That's all."

❂ ❂ ❂

"Good evening.

"A new poll suggests that Senator Cassie McClellan is in serious trouble, as recent revelations about her husband's sexual activities and the controversy over the public statements of Amber Stephens have put the Senator in a whole new light. In addition, the firings at the Crandall Corporation, which seem to go against the promises she made to the voters and the workers, have aroused additional antagonism against her.

"37% of voters now believe that she should resign her position in the United States Senate.

"34% believe she should stay in her job."

"27% weren't sure."

"39% believe that she stole the election."

"Ben Hansen, what do you think of all this?"

"Jim, even if her numbers go further south, she may have enough pride and guts to stick it out."

"No one's going to frighten her off."

"She's one tough cookie. I think she'll weather this storm."

"But it could become rough."

"No doubt it will."

❂ ❂ ❂

"Can Senator Cassie McClellan survive? That's the first question before the panel tonight on *Capital Currents*. Brock Cassidy?"

"Roy, I think she can. After all, she herself didn't do anything wrong. Her husband did, and he's going to have to pay the price—"

"Nonsense! They're linked—"

"Flora O'Herlihy?"

"They're tied together in the public's mind, and he was with her every step of the way. They sold themselves as a team—"

"But every woman will identify with her and sympathize—"

"Nicole DiBoneventura?"

"Every woman knows what it's like to have a jerk for husband, to be saddled with some overgrown adolescent who's a constant embarrassment. Right now he's her embarrassment, and most women will figure that she did what she could, but that he was simply a fool who couldn't control his own urges—"

"If she can't control her own husband—"

"Neil Gosselin, what's—"

"Then what *can* she do? This incident makes her look like a fool. What was going on in her house? Didn't she wonder where he was?"

"He had a difficult job—"

"Wasn't he ever home?"

"And what about the money?"

"What about it?"

"She's supposed to be a financial authority, with her eye on every penny that goes out of—"

"What does this have to do with the federal debt?"

"She's always said she watched their family budget—"

"He may have had his own account—"

"What did say she years ago about money and her family? 'If we can't afford something, we don't buy it—'"

"She didn't throw it away—"

"No, he did—"

"But it's her bankbook, too—"

"If she was paying attention—"

"Maybe she was too busy to notice. Or maybe she didn't care—"

"And maybe he had to get something on the outside he couldn't get at home—"

"That's low!"

"But it could be true."

"Even so—"

"All I know is that this report turns her into a complete hypocrite—"

"Or, even worse, a joke."

"Look, we know he's a skunk—"

"Who broke the law—"

"Right. But other candidates have survived this sort of thing—"

"Even when they put up that 'holier-than-thou' front?"

"Especially then."

"Right. They retreat under the umbrella of God's forgiveness—"

"She didn't do anything!"

"Just ignored her husband's shoddy behavior!"

"And now she's trying to excuse it!"

"Neil—"

"Don't worry. We're bound to learn more."

"How do you know?"

"Because we always learn more!"

"But how do you know?"

"Because the people who tried to protect her—"

"What people?"

"The unions. During the campaign, after her husband quit his job to support them, they moved to her side."

"And now?"

"They're fed up because they figure both McClellans lied to them. And that's why all this garbage has come out."

"You figure the unions stole these pages?"

"Of course!"

"And you expect further revelations?"

"That's the nature of the beast."

⊞ ⊞ ⊞

"I only said those things because he paid me."

"This is Jim Smathers. We interrupt our current program to bring you this statement from Amber Stephens, the woman at the center of the McClellan-Harrington controversy."

"—I met Philip McClellan when I was working out of Berkeley House. When he learned that I had been fired by Senator Harrington, he suggested that I should talk openly about my relationship with the Senator. He also agreed to pay me if I did."

"Why did you do it? Just for the money?"

"I was angry."

"In other words, you acted out of revenge."

"And for the money."

"Just to clarify: whose idea was it to make all those claims public?"

"Mr. McClellan's."

"Did he threaten you in any way?"

"No."

"Do you still insist that you had an affair with Senator Harrington?"

"Yes."

"Did the Senator ever say ever say he loved you?"

"Not in so many words."

"Did Mr. McClellan?"

"No."

"Did you believe then that Senator Harrington loved you?"

"Yes."

"Why?"

"I just did. A woman knows these things."

"Did Mr. McClellan add any details to your story?"

"No. He just listened, then told me what to say."

"How much did he pay you?"

"Twenty-five thousand dollars."

"Did you know that what you were doing was wrong?"

"I didn't care. I wanted to hurt Senator Harrington."

"When Mr. McClellan told you his plans, did he ever mention his wife?"

"Yes."

"Before that, when you were just . . . going together, did he ever mention her?"

"Yes."

"What did he say?"

"He said that she was busy with the campaign, and didn't have time for him, but that he wanted her to win because it would mean a lot for him personally."

"Did he explain any further?"

"We didn't talk that much."

"Did Mr. McClellan say that his wife was aware that he was paying you to make these accusations?"

"Yes."

"Did he say that she approved?"

"He said she was all for it, that she was looking for any way to give Senator Harrington trouble."

"Ms. Stephens, are you sorry for what you did?"

"Yes."

"Why are you revealing all this now?"

"Because people need to know the truth about Mr. McClellan. They also should know what kind of woman his wife is."

"What are your plans?"

"I'll answer that. I'm Kate Cosgrove, Ms. Stephens's attorney. We know that Ms. Stephens has acted badly. Nonetheless, we do not believe that any specific laws have been broken. Now, as we consider the possibility of charges against her, she will try to start her life over. Again, on behalf of my client, we regret all that has transpired."

"Amber, where will you go?"

"I'm not sure."

"Have you spoken to law enforcement officials?"

"My lawyer has."

"What charges do you expect?"

"I don't know."

"That's all. Thank you, ladies and gentlemen."

"Welcome back.

"We seem to have come to the end of the news conference. It also seems that for the time being, at least, we won't hear any more from doe-eyed Amber Stephens, who claims that she spread the now familiar story about her affair with Senator Vance Harrington at the suggestion of Philip McClellan, husband of Harrington's opponent at the time, the current Senator, Cassie McClellan, and the man whom she met at the Berkeley Bordello."

"And let's not forget the crucial part of her statement: she says she spoke with the full approval of the Senator herself."

"That may be the most important news of all."

"Exactly."

⊠ ⊠ ⊠

"I never suggested anything. She volunteered to tell her story."

"That's what Philip McClellan said at a news conference this afternoon, when he accused Amber Stephens of lying about their relationship at the Berkeley Bordello.

"Good evening, I'm Sue Konstacky.

"This afternoon, shortly after three o'clock, Mr. McClellan admitted that he saw Ms. Stephens socially, but he also claimed that the scheme to accuse former Senator Vance Harrington of having an affair with her was Ms. Stephens's own idea. Here's more from Mr. McClellan."

"When she learned who I was, she told me about her past and that she worked in Harrington's office. In fact, she told me a lot about him, his whole set-up."

"Is that when you asked whether the two of them had had an affair?"

"I didn't ask! She told me straight out."

"Why did she want to reveal all that information?"

"She said she wanted Harrington to lose."

"Did you tell her not to talk?"

"I didn't tell her anything."

"But did you—"

"She was determined to make what happened between the two of them public knowledge."

"Did she demand money right away?"

"No."

"When did you pay her?"

"After she made her first announcement, she demanded $10,000, or she said she'd bring me into it. The next time, she wanted 15,000 more."

"Why did you pay?"

"She said that if I didn't, she'd tell everyone under what circumstances we met. When, how, and everything else. I didn't want to hurt my wife and family, so I gave Ms. Stephens the money. I just hoped that she would take it and go away."

"But she didn't."

"No."

"Where did you get the money?"

"I have my own bank account."

"And your wife knew nothing about this?"

"I tried to protect her. It didn't work, but I tried."

"How do you feel now?"

"Now that everything's come out, I have nothing to hide and nothing to lose. I only hope that my indiscretions do not hurt my wife any more than they already have, because she had absolutely no knowledge of what I was doing."

"Are you saying that she didn't know that you paid Ms. Stephens?"

"Exactly."

"Ms. Stephens says your wife knew everything."

"Then she's lying."

"Do you—"

"Or confused. Either way, she's a very disturbed woman."

"Why would she reveal all this now?"

"You'll have to ask her."

"Can you think of any reason?"

"Maybe somebody got to her."

"In what sense—"

"Maybe someone threatened her."

"Are you saying somebody forced her to tell the truth?"

"Or her distorted version of it."

"Do you believe Senator Harrington had something to do with it?"

"I don't know."

"What does your wife think?"

"You'll have to ask her."

"What about Senator Harrington?"

"What about him?"

"Do you believe he had an affair with Amber Stephens?"

"I certainly think it's possible."

"He still denies any relationship with Ms. Stephens."

"Well, he would, wouldn't he?"

"Soon after that exchange, the press conference ended. Back to you, Sue."

"Ben, this is turning into a classic 'he said-she said.'"

"I guess so, but there's clearly at least one more twist to the story."

"What do you mean?"

"Well, it's more of a triangle, more of a 'he said-she said-he said.'"

"Or maybe a rectangle: a 'he said-she said-he said-she said.'"

"Either way, it may be the most complicated business I've ever heard."

"It sure is a mess. Stay on top of it, Ben."

"I wouldn't miss a moment."

"I'm sitting with former Senator Vance Harrington. Thanks for stopping by, Senator."

"Good to see you, Ben."

"I'm sure you've been following the news about Phil McClellan, Amber Stephens, and the rest."

"I'm keeping up."

"What's your reaction to what you've heard?"

"Like everybody else, I don't who or what to believe."

"How about Amber Stephens?"

"As I've always maintained, she remembers things far differently than I do."

"You're reaffirming again that you never had an affair with her."

"Exactly."

"No matter what she says."

"Right."

"And what about the role of the McClellans?"

"Frankly, nothing they say or do surprises me any more. They were willing to go to any lengths to win the election. I'll suppose they'll do anything to keep her job."

"Do you think Phil McClellan set up Amber, or did Amber use him?"

"I haven't the slightest idea."

"And what about the Senator? Where does she fit in?"

"She's just smart enough to play dumb."

"So you figure she knew everything."

"Right."

"Anything else?"

"Let's just say that they deserve each other."

"Fair enough. Any regrets about the campaign?"

"Sure."

"If you had the chance, what would you do differently?"

"Maybe I should have fought back even harder, but I have to tell you: it's late in the day for regrets."

"Thanks for your time."

"You're welcome."

"We resent any insinuation on the part of Mr. McClellan or anyone else that Ms. Stephens is unbalanced."

"These were the words of attorney Kate Cosgrove as she spoke today about her client, Amber Stephens, who is at the center of the controversy swirling about the husband of Senator Cassie McClellan.

"I'm Sue Konstacky, and this is *Channel 6 Action News*. Here's more from that encounter."

"Ms. Stephens was paid $25,000 by Mr. McClellan to speak about her affair with former Senator Harrington, and with Senator McClellan's full knowledge and approval, she did so. Now, to save himself as well as his wife's political career, Mr. McClellan has conceived this fantastic and unbelievable story: that making the accusation public was Ms. Stephens's idea."

"He says she originated the plot."

"Then he is lying."

"He says that she wanted to tell her story."

"Again, he is lying."

"He says his wife knew nothing about it."

"Once more, he is—"

"Then you claim that she was his dupe."

"We're not proud of the fact, but it's the truth."

"Doesn't she deserve some blame here?"

"Ms. Stephens accepts that blame."

"But—"

"Let me finish! Ms,. Stephen told the truth about her relationship with Senator Harrington, and she has no reason to apologize for that. Where Ms. Stephens went wrong was to become an accomplice of Senator and Mr. McClellan. Please remember, though, that the plan to make everything public was Mr. McClellan's creation. And Senator McClellan went along every step of the way."

"Is that Ms. Stephens's final story?"

"That's the truth."

"Any chance she'll say any more?"

"She is finished talking."

"I stand by my husband."

"That was United States Senator Cassie McClellan when she made a statement today in Washington.

"Here are more excerpts from that press conference."

"My husband has explained his relationship with Ms. Stephens. He also explained that he was only trying to protect me and our children, and I believe him."

"Senator, were you aware that Ms. Stephens was blackmailing him?"

"No."

"Were you aware that he had paid her money?"

"No."

"Did you know that Ms. Stephens was trying to get revenge on Senator Harrington?"

"I knew nothing about that. I knew only what she stated in public: that she felt used and rejected by him. I had no reason to doubt her."

"Do you doubt her now?"

"I'm not sure what Ms. Stephens knows or did. What I do suspect is that she has a very distorted perception of reality."

"Do you believe you owe Senator Harrington an apology?"

"No, because I still believe he cheated on his wife."

"So did your husband."

"My husband has taken full responsibility for his mistakes. I haven't heard Mr. Harrington apologize or do anything of the sort."

"He has always denied that he had an affair with Ms. Stephens."

"I know only what I've heard. And that's confusing enough."

"But—"

"Furthermore, his political ideals are still at odds with those of the vast majority of the American people."

"Then you feel the same way about him."

"Absolutely."

"Do you feel you were elected under false pretenses?"

"I was elected because of my values and beliefs. Those have not changed."

"Back to *Inside Entertainment*, and our rundown of the new shows for the upcoming season.

"The next one is called "Kidnapped," and it involves a family who suddenly discovers that one of their members has disappeared and must be found within twenty-four hours."

"Can they call the police?"

"No! That's part of the excitement."

"Sounds wild. Now here's another show: "And Now They're Free.""

"Ooooooh! Sounds scary!"

"It is. The show follows criminals recently released from prison, and films them as they try to work their way back into the community."

"Doesn't everyone know who they are?"

"No! And that's the fun. They only tell the truth at the end of the show!"

"Wow! So some people will think they've hired a regular employee for their business, only to find out they've hired a professional thief."

"Exactly! Or maybe they've hired a sex offender to take care of their children."

"Ooooooh! Sounds creepy!"

"We'll be right back."

⊠ ⊠ ⊠

"Good afternoon, everyone. Joe Lasher here, with another hour of truth, justice, and the American way.

"Well, those liberal pinheads are at it again. They've attacked a truly great American, Senator Cassie McClellan, and they're trying to make her resign.

"Folks, let me put your fears at ease. It ain't gonna happen. No way. No how. It simply ain't gonna happen.

"Let's review the facts. Senator McClellan's husband, Phil is his name, as if you don't know by now, got caught in a little hanky-panky. Right. He visited what they call the 'Berkeley Bordello.'

"Okay. We all know that this is not the best way for a man to spend his free time, but, hey, it's hardly the worst, either. A little frat boy folly. Nothing more than that.

"By the way, do liberals indulge in this same behavior? Of course they do! All the time! And a lot more often! You know they do! Their names are in the book!

"But do we hear about them? No, sir. Never. The only one we hear about is poor Phil McClellan.

"And what happens when he goes to this place? He meets a way-out whack-job named Amber Stephens, who was used and abused by that great hypocrite himself, Vance Harrington. And suddenly Phil finds himself in the middle of a mess.

"All right. It happens. You know the old line: Never play cards with a man called Doc, never eat at a place called Mom's, and never go to bed with anyone who has more problems than you do.

"Well, Phil went to bed with somebody who has a lot more problems, *a lot more problems*, than he does.

"Okay, he did something stupid. I admit it. But then we've all done stupid things. I have. Haven't you? Of course you have.

"But what does any of this have top do with Senator McClellan herself? Nothing. Absolutely nothing.

"Did she tell him to go there? No.

"Did she know when he went there? No.

"Did she know that Amber was going to tell her story about Vance Harrington? No. (And by the way, I believe Amber's story about him 100%.)

"Does any of this foolishness prevent her from being an effective legislator? Not at all.

"Is she still a pro-life, anti-tax, pro-growth, anti-government patriot? You bet she is!

"So let the liberals worry about Amber Stephens. Let the liberals focus on husband Phil. In the mean time, let's do our job and throw our support behind a great woman, Senator Cassie McClellan.

"She deserves everything she gets."

※ ※ ※

"He was given a $5 million golden parachute."

"Those were the astonishing words uttered by union boss Henry Warnacki at the Crandall Corporation today.

"Good evening. I'm Sue Konstacky."

"The incredible story of this year's election for United States Senate took one more bizarre twist today, when it was learned that Phil McClellan, husband of Senator Cassie McClellan, accepted a $5 million payoff when he resigned from the company last year. Here with more is Cindy Howell."

"Thanks, Sue. I'm sure everyone remembers that sensational moment when Phil McClellan resigned from Crandall, citing the unfair treatment of union workers:

"That is why I have just resigned from Crandall. Apparently my presence has prevented the two sides from achieving a solution. In fact, my fighting for the rights of workers may have caused the Board's position to harden. If management is indeed using me as a scapegoat, my resignation might ease tensions and salvage jobs. I certainly hope so."

"When he made this statement, many observers regarded it as the turning point in the election. Until then, Senator McClellan, who had spoken out so often against what she called the subversive influence of unions, was the target of their anger. But after Mr. McClellan resigned, sympathies went to both husband and wife. And on Election Day, so did the votes.

"Today, however, given the spate of massive firings at Crandall, and now this announcement, such sentiment is sure to change. If the story is true, then Phil McClellan's resignation was a sham, as well as a way for him and his wife to change the public's perception so she could win the election.

"We're all waiting for answers from the McClellans. Both of them. Cindy Howell, *Channel 6 Action News*."

"Thanks, Cindy.

"Wow. The election . . . and the story . . . that never ends. Ben Hansen is sitting with me. What's your reaction, Ben?"

"Sue, this is an amazing revelation."

"Did anyone expect it?"

"I'll be honest. I didn't."

"Nor did I. But . . . where do we go from here?"

"Well, obviously the first thing we have to find out is whether this claim is true."

"That's number one. And what's your gut feeling?"

"It may be. It just may be."

"And then?"

"I want to know how Mr. Warnacki obtained this information. Where did it come from?"

"You want to know his source."

"Exactly. Was it someone from the management side who was angry with either one of the McClellans?"

"Or was it a union official?"

"Or was it someone we haven't even considered?"

"Like an office worker. Or a guy on the line."

"It could have come from anywhere, because . . . let's face it . . . and I don't enjoy saying this . . . both McClellans have piled up a lot of enemies."

"What do you mean?"

"The union people feel betrayed by the firings, so they'd be glad to give the McClellans all the problems they can."

"And management?"

"Management may feel as if they've been used. They're also not thrilled with her recent support for fired workers, including her attacks on management."

"Wow. Of course, we have yet to hear from either Cassie or Phil McClellan."

"And until we do, we'd better withhold judgment."

"And we will. But let's take this one step further."

"Okay."

"Let's suppose that the rumor is not true."

"You mean, suppose no money was involved."

"Right."

"Then we need to find out who released such an outrageous lie."

"Fair enough. But now . . . suppose it is true."

"If Phil McClellan did receive that $5 million . . . then the demands for his wife's resignation will only grow louder."

"Thanks, Ben. We'll be right back."

"She's toast, Roy. Done. Gone. Wrap her up with a pretty ribbon, tie it into a bow, and send her on her way."

"You're saying her career in politics is finished."

"Over. Caput. Finis. We're counting the hours toward resignation."

"Brock Cassidy?"

"Not necessarily, Roy. She still may not have known about the gift—"

"Are you kidding me—"

"Flora O'Herlihy?"

"How could she not know about $5 million?"

"What kind of a fool is she—"

"I don't think she's a fool at all—"

"He might have socked it away on his own—"

"Nicole—"

"Men do that kind of thing all the time."

"I'm sure they do, but how often can she plead ignorance—"

"C'mon—"

"And if she does, I guarantee you the American people will give her another chance—"

"Certainly the women will—"

"We're a very forgiving people—"

"Forget it! If she wasn't a joke before, she certainly is one now—"

"She is still a United States Senator—"

"In name only—"

"We need more evidence—"

"Only you do, Brock—"

"The American people will demand it—"

"They'll get it—"

"When?"

"Any minute now."

"Is that a prediction or a prayer?"

"Both. With all the sex stuff—"

"Everybody's forgotten about that—"

"Only you, Brock."

"The rest of the world remembers every word—"

"We're talking about lies here—"

"From who?"

"The McClellans behaved despicably. Both of 'em."

"No matter how strongly she denies—"

"Let's not rush to judgment—"

"I say she should start cleaning out her office. And good riddance."

"Tough talk from Neil Gosselin. We'll be back to *Capital Currents* in a minute."

⊞ ⊞ ⊞

"New worries for Senator McClellan.

"In a stunning revelation today, the CEO of the Crandall Corporation, R. Henry Carteret, spoke about Senator Cassie McClellan at the company's headquarters."

"—apparently Senator's McClellan's memory tends to fail quite often these days, as she claims to be unaware of the financial settlement between her husband and the Crandall Corporation.

"Well, I suppose a few thousand dollars might have slipped by. I can't imagine, though, that she has lost total recall of the down payment of another several hundred thousand that we provided for her family's new house in Cancun. All of these monies were part of the termination agreement with Philip McClellan."

"Sir—"

"Just a moment, and I'll take questions."

"Did you know that she—"

"In a moment! Lately Senator McClellan has become particularly angry with Crandall, apparently to boost her own political standing. May I remind her that we are the ones who helped her get elected.

"Now I'll take questions."

"Sir, how much money are you talking about?"

"Are you speaking of the down payment on the house?"

"Yes."

"Roughly $678,000."

"And is there any doubt in your mind that Senator McClellan knew about this sum as part of her husband's termination package?"

"None whatsoever."

"The question went on a for several more minutes, but here was the key part of this remarkable assertion. For instant analysis, we turn to Ben Hansen."

"Hello, Jim."

"Good evening, Ben. I'll put everything right on the line. What will the impact be of this latest disclosure?"

"Jim, if it's true, and we caution everyone that we have yet to hear the Senator's response, if it's true . . . I can't see how she remains an effective public servant. The charge of collusion, the outright lies, it's all too much for anyone to explain."

"Why would the Crandall Corporation take part in such a scheme?"

"That's easy, Jim. They wanted a powerful ally in-state and in Washington, and Mrs. McClellan definitely filled the bill."

"Do you think she'll have to resign?"

"Absolutely. And, let me add, sooner rather than later."

⁂

"Turmoil in the Senate!

"Welcome to *Capital Currents*. Well, the knives are out for Senator Cassie McClellan, who has become the target of several investigations into her finances and political operations. Brock Cassidy, what do you think?"

"Roy, she's in for a few hot weeks, maybe even a couple of hot months—"

"More like sweltering—"

"But she's just one more example of liberal hostility toward a female conservative who doesn't fit their image of how a woman should act and think."

"Oh, c'mon—"

"Will she survive?"

"I'd never count her out."

"Flora O'Herlihy, you've been chomping at the bit—"

"Roy, this woman has told enough lies and left a trail of such distortion and downright deception—"

"Pretty fancy wordplay there, Flora—"

"It was only a matter of time before they caught up with her, and now she's getting back what she deserves—"

"I've never heard such nonsense—"

"Nicole DiBoneventura—"

"She's made a few slips—"

"A few!"

"And she's suffered a couple of memory lapses—"

"She lied over and over—"

"And now the leftwing media and their stooges in the Congress and elsewhere have resolved to take revenge on a woman—"

"Who are you trying to kid?"

"– who simply stands up for what she believes—"

"She got elected by crooked—"

"Neil Gosselin?"

"She ran a crooked campaign, she's been a crooked and corrupt Senator, and now her entire career is being used against her!"

"If a man did any of these things, he'd be—"

"Out the window a long time ago!"

"Nobody would say a word."

"They'd slaughter him! In fact, it's only because she's a woman—"

"She fought for her ideals—"

"She smeared her opponent—"

"She told the truth—"

"She operated strictly by innuendo—"

"Don't you love with way she forgave her husband so quickly—"

"She's not responsible for him—"

"Sure, sure, she had no idea what was going on—"

"I agree. He's a snake—"

"And she knew everything he was doing—"

"Even if she did—"

"She did—"

"That doesn't mean she's guilty—"

"She's guilty of lying and stealing and accepting money—"

"Bottom line—"

"She's a national embarrassment—"

"Bottom line—"

"She's a victim—"

"BOTTOM LINE! Will she survive?"

"Yes."

"No."

"Yes."

"No."

"The correct answer? Too close to call."

"An extraordinary political moment.

"Good evening. I'm Sue Konstacky.

"It was hardly unexpected, but the drama was still powerful, as Senator Cassie McClellan, not long ago regarded as one of the rising stars in the Conservative firmament, came home to bid farewell to friends and supporters. Here with more is Cindy Howell."

"Sue, the tone was a mixture of anger and resignation, as Cassie McClellan offered what may be her valedictory address."

"I have been proud to serve my community and my country. I have been proud to fight for the cause and the values which we all uphold.

"But events of the last months have made it impossible for me to continue. And I refuse to let my husband and my children endure any more pain than they have.

"Did I make mistakes? I suppose so. My husband and I both have committed actions and spoken words that we regret. As a result, we ourselves have suffered grievous pain, and part of our efforts over the upcoming period will be to dedicate ourselves to each other and to our family. We still have a lot of love to share.

"But I cannot leave office without reaffirming my belief that we have been persecuted by the media, by the liberal-dominated Washington culture that did everything it could to undermine us. And you, too.

"Maybe they resented me as a woman.

"Maybe they resented a woman who proudly espouses conservative values.

"Maybe they simply hate all conservatives, at least those who won't compromise in the face of liberal attacks.

"Whatever the reason, we became victims of a brutal political culture.

"But please, no tears for us. We'll carry on, and we'll fight with you and others to make our country great again. And one day, with your efforts, and with a firm reliance on God's grace, we will win.

"Thank you."

"Sue, the cheers that followed those words rang out for a long time. Ms. McClellan didn't take any questions, and she didn't specify what her immediate plans might be, but for the time being I think it's safe to say that she will retreat to her home, where she and her husband will try to put their shattered lives back together. Cindy Howell, *Channel 6 Action News*."

"Thanks, Cindy.

"Well, comment all over our area and throughout Washington was dominated by reaction to the McClellan resignation, but perhaps the most interesting comment came from McClellan's opponent in the last campaign, former Senator Vance Harrington, who spoke from Acapulco Mexico, where he is vacationing."

"As bitter as our battles were, I cannot react to Ms. McClellan's resignation with anything but sadness. One, our region has lost an aggressive and determined representative. I admit that I rarely agreed with her on any issue, but I respected her passion, and her willingness to fight for the cause she advocated. Two, I always feel sorry when families suffer because one member takes on him or herself the burdens of a political career. But I trust that the McClellans and their children will emerge from this crisis stronger than ever."

"I should add that as many of you know, Senator Harrington is currently on his honeymoon with his third wife, former legislative aide Elaine Corbett, who left the Harrington campaign under a cloud of allegations about extra-marital behavior. The two were married just weeks ago.

"We'll be right back."

⊠ ⊠ ⊠

"Today I announce my intention to run for the office of United States Senator."

"Good evening. I'm Jim Smathers.

"It didn't take long for the next campaign to get underway, as a challenge has stepped up to compete for the Senate seat vacated just weeks ago by Cassie McClellan. Here's Cindy Howell."

"Jim, Frederick Dorman, newly elected conservative Congressman, jumped right in today to attempt, in his words, 'to fill the void left by the great Cassie McClellan.'"

"Her cause has become my cause.

"You know what I stand for: lower taxes, less government interference, preserving the rights of the unborn, saving marriage, improving education, creating jobs, and altogether restoring American respect throughout the world!"

"Yay!"

"Let's take this country back!"

"Yay!"

"Let's rebuild the America you and I love!"

"Yay!"

"Are you with me?"

"YAY!"

"Good! Then let's go to work!"

"Jim, the crowds were certainly enthusiastic. Whether Mr. Dorman can ever arouse passion similar to that achieved by former Senator McClellan is open to speculation, but he's certainly made clear that he intends to appeal to the same group of voters. Cindy Howell, *Channel 6 Action News*."

"Thanks, Cindy.

"In a related story, former Senator Cassie McClellan has been hired as a commentator for the Nationwide News Network. According to a statement released today, 'Senator McClellan will offer unique and personal insights into the key issues of our time.'

"Ms. McClellan has also accepted a multi-million dollar advance from Rillington Publishers, another division of the Nationwide Corporation, to write a book about her experiences in and out of politics, tentatively titled *Courage and Beyond*.

"We'll be right back."

About the Author

VICTOR L. CAHN is Professor of English at Skidmore College, and the author of five books on Shakespeare; critical volumes on Tom Stoppard and Harold Pinter; *Conquering College: A Guide for Undergraduates*; the memoir *Classroom Virtuoso*; and the novel *Romantic Trapezoid*. His articles and reviews have appeared in such varied publications as *The New York Times*, *The Literary Review*, *Modern Drama*, *The Chronicle of Higher Education*, and *Variety*. He has written numerous plays, including several produced Off-Broadway as well as regionally: *Roses in December*; *Embraceable Me*; *Fit to Kill* (all published by Samuel French); *Getting the Business*; *Dally with the Devil*; *Sheepskin/Bottom of the Ninth*; and *Sherlock Solo*, a one-man show that he performs. He has also played leading roles in works by Shakespeare, Pinter, Coward, Simon, Gurney, and Knott.